The Rise and Fall of Millicent

I0685365

Daryn Cross

ISBN: 0615827969
ISBN-13: 978-0615827964

DARYN CROSS

THE RISE AND FALL OF MILLICENT

BY DARYN CROSS

MILLICENT

Chapter One

1875, Millwood, New York

"Millicent you better get your little fanny here now, or so help me, I'll beat you until you can't see. Stop hiding, girl, just because your brother got a beating. It won't save you. I have a belt and you'll have stripes across your back."

Mil hid under the house in the small milk room that few entered this time of day. She trembled as she clutched her baby doll. "Francine, I will never beat you, honey. I swear, not one mark will ever be on you. I'll protect you like Mama can't."

She heard her mother arguing with her father above her. The slaps resounded across her space. A dull thud hit the floor. She scrunched up her eyes, trying to think of something else. Something happy like Mama had taught her. *Think summer and the lake is there, not cold but warm and inviting. We're taking a boat ride, Mil. Don't you see the birds in the air?*

"I think David's okay, Fran," she told the doll. "He was just lying there to keep Daddy from hitting him again." She wept, holding her doll in her hands.

"Jason, so help me God. You touch me one more time and I'll…"

Millicent cried some more into Fran's crinoline. Mama was being strong. Mama was holding her own.

Whack!

She shook.

Whack, whack!

Millicent, clutched the doll in her balled up fists. "She'll be okay. Just like David. It'll be all right. You'll see."

"Where did you get that Marilyn? Don't point that at me. You don't think I was serious? I was just trying to make you understand…"

The gun went off. Three times.

Millicent held her hands over her ears. "Don't listen Fran." *It'll be okay. . .*

She woke up and didn't know how long she'd slept. Grit in her eyes, Millicent clutched Francine in her arms. It was pitch black.

"Mil, are you in there?"

"Mama?"

Her Mother sobbed. "Come here, sweet potato, I need you. You need me. We'll be okay."

Okay? Maybe. But she'd never trust a man again, especially one like her Papa.

Chapter Two

1887, New York City

"Millicent, come to the table dear. Time for breakfast."

She rolled her eyes and lifted her head from her book. "Mother, I am still reading *Jane Eyre*."

"Get your nose out of that book. Now! Honestly, Bart, the girl is going to turn into a shriveled up old maid if we do not take steps to remedy it."

That got her attention. She slammed the book shut and placed it on the side table. She jumped up from the settee and quickly made her way through the foyer, around the stairs, and into the kitchen. She faced her parents like a soldier ready to do battle. "I do not plan to marry."

Neither spoke, and she continued to stare at her mother, daring the woman to contradict her words. Surely Mama, who'd suffered as bad as she had in the past, could not have forgotten the way Father had treated them all. He'd killed her only brother. If one could report anything good coming from the experience, it would be that due to her brother's death and their position in society Mama was released from a murder charge. Not that it mattered, because the stupid woman, doing what a sane person would consider incomprehensible, had entered into yet another marriage, this time to a mealy-mouthed old man at least fifteen years her senior.

"And what do you plan to do, Millicent?" Bart's beady eyes bore through her, black and menacing.

She sucked in her breath. The man hated her. The feeling was mutual. He was pompous, irritatingly high-maintenance, women were to be at his beck-and-call, and the man was forever putting her down. She swallowed a lump in her throat. At least he didn't make a habit of beating people. Her mother had taught her to see the good in every human, no matter how fleeting. Because in the end, to her, Bart Haverford solidified her belief about all men. They were inferior, and compensated for their failings by demeaning the women around them. If she ever had the chance to assume a position of power, men would never have the upper hand again.

"I plan to be a Governess." She smiled. "For a man who has no wish to stay at home and will leave me to tend to matters."

"There is no way you will ever find a job like that." He held his belly and hooted.

The raucous sound of his laughter made her want to spew. "Such positions do exist." She stared down at the floor.

"In books by authors from England." Her mother smiled. "Darling, I know you covet your total freedom, but a time comes in every young woman's life when she must do the right thing."

In spite of herself, Millicent snorted. "The right thing? Mother how could you even suggest you know what that is for me? Is it the right thing to hand over your body to a man who wishes to do nothing but abuse it, both from overwork and his lascivious needs?"

"Don't be impertinent, young lady." Bart arched an eyebrow. "A normal woman cleaves to a man, but perhaps you will never be normal. Nevertheless, you shall not speak to your mother in such a manner, *and* you will not contradict our plans to ensure you are well-taken care of. You dare not bring disrespect to your mother's or my family. For your refusal could require me to toss your spoiled, little bratty self into the streets. I doubt then anyone would hire you even for a Governess."

As her gut twisted in a knot, Millicent felt like she was sinking into a black void. "Plans? What plans?"

Mama placed her hand on Millicent's shoulder. "A

young man is in need of a wife. His father has spoken with Bart and they have agreed to an arranged marriage. The gentleman in question, though somewhat spirited himself, has agreed to the union as long as you are not…" She turned to her husband. "What was the phrase, Bart?"

He chuckled as he set down his cup. "Ugly as a witch or long in the tooth." He glared at Millicent. "I assured William that you are somewhat pleasing to look at, not entirely plain, and that you are of suitable age. Eighteen is perfect."

"So *you* think." *What a horse's arse. I'd like to see him waiting on another human being and subjected to spread his legs to have someone's crying imp.* "A Governess should attend an institute of higher learning and I do not appreciate being sold."

"Millicent!" Her mother placed both hands on Mil's shoulders. "Apologize to your stepfather. He only has your best interests at heart."

She scoffed at her mother's naiveté. "No doubt there's something in it for him."

Sneering at her, he socked his fist into his palm. She smiled inwardly. Thank the heavens the man was not violent by nature, for there was no doubt she'd angered him to the point of wishing he were. It was her silent badge of honor to provoke him.

"I am bound to have a dowry to give to William, of

course. I would not be honorable otherwise, not that I consider you worth as much as I shall have to give. He, of course, being much better off financially than we, has told me he refuses to make this one-sided."

She narrowed her eyes. "Translation, you have another business deal."

***

Millicent sat on her bed, dressed in a pale green tea gown, and wished she were dead. Her mother and that hideous man had not even given her a reprieve from her sentence, hurrying it along as if she must be drawn and quartered by midnight. Surely to be so would be a more humane death than to die by inches over countless years of servitude.

He was coming to tea. She was certain he was, but not to socialize. William Davis, Junior was coming to examine his potential merchandise. Her breeding and appropriate demeanor. She'd make sure she opened her mouth so he could determine that all her teeth were present and accounted for. If she dared, she'd make a mockery of this meeting, make the man shy off and not claim possession. His word was the final say while she had no rights whatsoever. The mere thought of it made steam figuratively rise from her head. Who made a man king of his palace?

"Because women were ignorant enough to allow

themselves to give birth," she muttered as she hit the mattress in anger. But not her. She wasn't pumping out any children unless it benefited her as she saw fit. Not for a man to pleasure himself and not for his pride to claim an heir. He'd pay in some way should she acquiesce to burdening herself.

The sudden knock on her door made her jump and reminded her of a funeral dirge. Apparently it had come time for her to meet the man to whom she eventually would sell her soul. Probably tomorrow if her stepfather had any say in the matter. She only hoped her intended betrothed was not ancient or had bow legs. Additionally, if she had to spread her legs at some point, which she planned to avoid until she could no longer, she only hoped he had enough to place between them and it wasn't limp.

She rose and checked her appearance in the bureau mirror, smoothing down one errant piece of red hair, and walked slowly to the door. Opening it, she nodded to her mother. "It was nice knowing you," she whispered and marched solemnly forward.

Millicent descended the stairs and turned right to the parlor. A man sat on their pale yellow Medallion sofa with his back to the entrance. Her stepfather stood when he saw her come through the archway. "William, here is my daughter, Millicent."

Daughter? She gagged. Her connection to the

10

avaricious toad was close enough as it was. The man on the sofa stood and turned. She glanced up at him. He was tall and broad-shouldered. Dark brown wavy hair framed his face. His eyes were pale, blue or green. She wasn't sure yet. She was certain he was far better looking than she'd hoped he would be. Trying hard not to believe her luck, Millicent crossed the room. When he opened his mouth, then she'd know without a doubt what his true colors were.

Curtseying in front of him, she held out her hand. "It is a pleasure to have you in our home, Mr. Davis." Okay, so she knew her manners if nothing else.

He took her hand in his, and for a moment, she could swear she felt a current. It made her giddy. He bent, pressed his lips to it, and her skin tingled. The room became unbelievably hot. "It is my pleasure to make your acquaintance, Miss Haverford."

Her face burned. "I beg your pardon, Mr. Davis, but my surname is actually Robinson. I am Mr. Haverford's stepdaughter."

Bart laughed nervously. "Yet we have a father-daughter relationship. Young waif lost her father when she was six."

Thankfully. And you, you miserable overbearing bore, had the grace to leave us alone for three years. Why wasn't it more? "Yes, I am afraid it was a serious accident." *He stood in front of a weapon and accepted three bullets to the head.* She smiled her sweetest.

"I see." The man's eyes, iridescently blue as she could now tell, dipped to the bodice of her dress. Her bosom heaved. "Pardon me for my error."

Oh I think I could pardon you for a lot of things. She began to reconsider the whole spreading the legs matter. "It is of no consequence, kind sir. Anyone would have erred so."

"Well." Bart rubbed his hands together, no doubt excited about his upcoming coup. "I'll just leave you two here in the parlor to get better acquainted and Mrs. Haverford will serve tea in the dining room on the hour."

"Have a seat," William told her as Bart raced from the room. "A gentleman always stands until a lady is properly settled."

She eased onto the side of the curve-backed sofa and he did the same on the other side. "I was rather surprised this morning when Mama and Bart told me of your wish." She attempted to bat her eyelashes. It seemed forward and a bit trite. Mama had been insistent it was a common occurrence.

He cleared his throat. "Pardon me, Miss Robinson, for being frank with you. I find that honesty is always the best policy."

She nodded. "As do I. Pray continue."

"This was not my idea." He exhaled as he rubbed the

back of his neck. "My father was insistent that I had reached the age where I needed a wife to appear planted and not taken as a dandy. Business requires that a man shows he is solid and responsible."

His words stung and she reeled as if she'd been slapped. "Of course. I momentarily forgot I was being auctioned off to the highest bidder."

His eyes widened and she cursed herself silently. Her mouth was always known for spouting off at precisely the incorrect moment.

"I did not mean my statement a demeaning remark. You are quite an attractive woman, Miss Robinson. Not many women have hair the color of a new copper penny, but I am not prepared to have an amorous relationship with a woman at this time."

She jutted out her chin as her stubborn streak grew bolder. "Pray tell when you believe your time will come?"

He sighed. "How does one predict such a thing? I tell you this because circumstances have brought us together in such a way that I believe I should fully disclose my intentions prior to a marriage contract. I do not want you to believe there will be favors I cannot bestow at this time."

Her body trembled with repressed anger. "Of course. Your will is in your control, for I never planned this to be a romantic tryst, but a business arrangement. My concern

13

has been that you would wish me to perform duties I did not care to perform."

His face lost all tension. Even the set of his shoulders appeared more relaxed. "Then, my dear Miss Robinson, we shall get along well. I have a full staff of servants waiting for a new mistress. There is no common housework for you to perform. There will be no concern over children or wifely requirements. I will ask that you only take my arm and attend public affairs. Simply appear as a wife would in more intimate circumstances, but only as normally would be viewed in genteel society."

"I can do that, Mr. Davis." She forced a smile.

He took her hand into his. "Then I believe we can let your family know we have come to agreement on marriage. May I call you Millicent?"

"And I shall address you as William."

He grinned for the first time. "I can't tell you how happy this makes me."

She returned his smile, refusing to appear as grim as she felt. "This makes me happy as well." *For now.*

Chapter Three

Millicent stood in front of the mirror in her wedding dress, stock still and unable to fathom how she got here. Over the course of the past few months, William had courted her for all outside eyes and ears, while their moments alone had consisted of mundane chatter and long periods of solitude.

She often wished she had stowed away a book within the folds of her gown for the times he was lost in studying his papers about an upcoming business deal or the new findings of a scientific mind. He never asked her to share or give her opinion, which she believed to be shortsighted. She was a well-educated woman, trained at one of the best schools, and spoke three languages fluently. She also was well-read in both fiction and select volumes of non-fiction. Science was a subject she relished; certain new developments would change their world as they knew it.

William, on the other hand, preferred to stick to political science, economics and business law, all of which bored her beyond the dollars and cents made. Who cared what theory caused public and private enterprise to function as they did?

Their outings went on far longer than she would have liked, William finally agreeing to set a date for the wedding. She was pleased to know that typically the charade in public was not as prominent once the marriage vows were made and was greatly relieved that respite was near at hand. Still she was aware a new tension would assume the space.

"You look, beautiful, Mil." Mama touched her shoulder, smiling, yet looking far older than her thirty-eight years warranted. Millicent wondered if the premature aging were a matter of genes. Would she fall prey to the same rotten luck? If only she could stay young forever.

"William Davis is a fortunate man." Her mother squeezed Millicent's hands. "Remember, tonight when you go to the marriage bed, he will want to consummate the marriage. It will hurt, dear. Men are sometime rough and unthinking. It will not last long, but there will be bleeding."

She exhaled as if remembering her own first wedding night. "I can tell William is fond of you and shall wish to ease your pain. Do not judge your intimacy based on one encounter, for, in time, the pain ceases, and you can have much pleasure with the right person." Her face showed no pleasure, however. "With the right person, of course."

Millicent's heart went out to her mother. At that moment, she realized Mama had never known that pleasure. First she was with a man who abused his relationship, more than likely getting what he wanted while leaving her still needing. Second she was now with a man who, without a shadow of a doubt, had no lasting power, if he could even start. All she could do was pacify her mother now by allowing her to believe her only daughter would possess that which had been denied to her. "I know what occurs, Mama. I have read about it. Do not worry."

"I should have monitored your reading material more closely. Perhaps now it is a good thing." Her mother hugged her. "I love you."

You may be the only one who ever does. She closed her eyes and willed the tears away. "I love you too, Mama."

***

The wedding was over. She breathed a sigh of relief as they pulled away in their small, yet grand carriage. "All seemed pleased."

He nodded. "Indeed. Your father especially. I've never seen a man smile so broadly. He must really love you."

He loves your father's money. "Oh I'm sure he's satisfied with today's result." She faced him. "Perhaps you should

17

begin by telling me the facts. What are my responsibilities once we are at your estate?"

He nervously adjusted his cravat. "You are a remarkable woman, Millicent, more business in your demeanor than many of my associates."

She nodded. "Women do not have to be mere chattel void of brains rattling in their heads. I dare say I have the mind to assist your business in ways you never imagined."

He nodded. "It appears you might. I shall consider how best to incorporate you into my affairs." A hint of a smile passed his lips. "Business enterprises of course."

A cold chill ran down her spine as her intuition kicked in. Could it be conceivable that William was hiding a secret he did not wish for her to know? Surely, he had no lover on the side? For to do so would be disastrous in the early stages of his career. If gossipmongers didn't hang him, no matter. She was capable of killing him with no questions asked. She smiled. His money and no man. Not a terrible prospect. Unfortunately, the times demanded she make him her mouthpiece. "Do not hesitate to call for my assistance."

At his home, the servants welcomed her, smiling and attentive. "Let me show you to your room, Mistress Davis," Grayson, William's manservant said. "The upstairs quarters await your approval." He led her up the stairs to a door. Opening it, he smiled. "Your suite."

She gasped. The eloquence was more than she'd expected. Silk tapestries hung from the walls. Elegant draperies adorned the nearly floor-to-ceiling windows. Then there was the bed, monstrous and on a platform in the middle of the room. The sheets shone in the candlelight, proclaiming they were fine silk, as did the coverlet above them. "This is breathtaking."

He nodded, obviously pleased with her statement. "This is Madam's room and Master's adjoins it." He nodded, knowing. "For yours and his easy access, of course."

Her heart broke. William had told her it would be so, yet the sight of the dual quarters solidified the reality of what would become her lonely existence. "I am certain it will do for that which is intended." She smiled in a confidence she knew to be false as she spoke the words.

"Of course, madam." He clicked his heels and left the room.

Hell, even the butler knew her statement was ludicrous. "I will make you change your mind, William." She folded her arms as she deliberated on her best plan.

***

Having left the door to William's room slightly ajar to ensure she waked, she heard him enter in the wee hours of the morning. Millicent wore the diaphanous nightshirt her mother had made for the wedding night, though she

19

normally slept nude. Deciding the shirt gave her allure, she left it on and slipped to the door, peaking around it as she watched William remove his clothing, one item at a time. He was weaving back and forth as he did so and muttering to himself in the process. With a quiet gasp, she realized he'd been into the spirits. No doubt drowning out the memory of wedding her. She bit her bottom lip. If only she could convince him she could be bewitching, warm and sensual in his arms.

As he removed every stitch of cloth from his body, she gazed upon his naked frame in wonder and overwhelming need. His shaft was large and body firm. Every bit as much the man as the statue of David, yet his penis much larger. If the books she'd read were correct, it could be larger still.

Slipping in quietly, Millicent clasped her arms around him from behind and caressed his stomach. "I was waiting for you to come to bed." She rubbed her breasts, barely clad in the wafer thin fabric across his back and jutted her pelvis, grinding it into his backside.

William jolted at her touch. "Millicent, I told you your wifely responsibilities were not required."

"What if I gladly accept them?" She let her hand drop to his shaft and rubbed lightly across it.

He shivered, his body reacting to her touch. "It is not right to have a sexual connection when I feel no emotion for you. I have nothing to give other than carnal pleasure. It does not feel right to treat you so. It would make me untrue to myself." He stumbled where he was.

Millicent steadied him and grabbed his cock in her hand and, for once in her life, felt the power of being in control, she in the dominant role and he as the weaker sex. His erection was magnificent as she rubbed down the length of him. Moisture gathered between her legs and she panted with the desire to feel him in her. "There is nothing wrong with taking me," she said huskily. "It is your right as my husband. My right to enjoy as a wife."

His breath came out close to a sob. "But I have not truly given myself to you, only made it legal. To me in the eyes of God we are still two and not as one."

"You made the vows in a church, William." She slid her hand down him once more. "Yet I do not care anymore. I want to know what it feels like. To be swept away in a haze, knowing a passion I have never felt, reaching the heights I have only read about in novels."

He turned in her arms, still shaking, his cock pressing her in her stomach. One hand reached up under her nightshirt and slid along her thigh. She opened her legs a bit to accommodate him while smiling at him, her eyes locked with his. He reeked strongly of alcohol. She ignored it as his fingers found their mark. As he flicked across her clitoris, it was she who shivered this time. Her legs quivered violently with desire for more.

"You are very wet, Millicent," he said, his voice low and slightly garbled. "I can smell your excitement."

"I need more than your hand."

He began to flick his finger across her delicate spot some more. As he did, spirals of heat gathered and there was tightness that coiled inside her threatening to ignite.

She reached down again and grabbed his cock. "This. This is what I need."

He grabbed her by the shoulders and pushed her to the floor. "Lie prone," he commanded.

This time she let him take charge, suddenly fearful of what she'd asked for. She had never suspected to lose her virginity like this.

He hovered over her, then grabbed her legs and spread them father apart. He pulled her legs up a bit in his hands, and then drove into her. Full and complete. She screamed out in pain as if he'd split her in two. He didn't seem to even hear her discomfort as he rode her as he would his prize horse. Pumping, pumping. She screamed again in pain. As she did, a magical thing happened as the pain subsided. But so did he, as he fell off her and passed out on the rug.

Millicent jumped to her feet, shaking. *Pleasure like hell. Torture.* The man was too large for her. He would never do that to her again. She stared at the blood spilled on his floor. So be it. Let him clean it up. No doubt at the same time he had to clean his vomit when he woke.

She strode quickly to the door of the adjoining room and closed it, taking the key with her to lock him out. As if she'd have to worry. She doubted he'd even be awake in time for breakfast.

***

Staring at her reflection in the mirror the next morning, Millicent was horrified at the dark circles under her eyes. No doubt because she'd been bled dry. She'd already washed up with her pitcher and basin, not prepared for the contraption that was available to her for more complete bathing. Her appearance would be what it was for now.

Trying to appear cheerful, she marched down the stairs, dressed in one of her new gowns, also purchased by her mother for her transition. She shouldn't have wasted the money or the time, for Millicent doubted this whole situation would be long term.

She entered the dining area to see the butler, Joseph, in attendance and no one else present. "I see I am the only one here for now."

"The only one here at all." Joseph held the teapot. "Would you like some Mistress?"

She nodded. "Please. Has William already left?" Her eyes widened, for she was positive he would not have resumed consciousness yet.

"Before daybreak. He asked that you forgive him for leaving without seeing his new bride but said he had business he had to attend to in Philadelphia."

Now her eyes were really open. "Philadelphia? But that is a long distance."

He nodded. "Master William said he will be gone a fortnight."

She closed her eyes and swore to herself. Damn the man. He had battered her and left without one real apology for his actions. Never mind him. She should have known better and would in the future. For now it was her life's work to discover why he avoided her so.

***

William rode his steed and wondered how he'd ever been talked into marrying such a willful woman when he'd wished to wed no one. Yet, weak as he was, he'd submitted to his father's pressure and done so. To make matters worse, he'd succumbed to watering down his misery in more than a pint of Scotch. For a man not used to drinking frequently, it was like a gallon. Then he'd displayed the supreme weakness by sacrificing his morals.

He rode the horse slowly over the hills to his destiny and swore in the early fog-filled air. Now he was shamed, hung over and barely able to function after only four hours of sleep. No more. From now on, he would be his own man.

What am I going to say to Juliana? How can I even face her now? His mind filled with the beauty of his love. Her golden eyes and chestnut hair, kissed with the gold highlights only the sun can bestow. Her scent wafted over him as if she were there, lilac and vanilla, fresh and pure and…not at all as he was now. He kicked the horse to move at a trot. It was better to get this over with. For to waste any more time was only delaying the inevitable.

"Why wasn't *she* suitable to be my wife?" he'd asked his father, as if the man were present. Yes, he knew she was orphaned and now lived alone in a small cottage in the country. No, she had no real money, making what she needed for food and clothing and taking in sewing to make a meager sum to pay for other things. Was being poor and a hard worker somehow a crime? Better that than spoiled, willful and a tease like Millicent.

Still to his father, the answer had been clear. "You have no idea who has had his hand under that woman's skirt, William. She lives near no one. There may be steady traffic to her cottage. If you truly have not bedded her, than you have no way of knowing if she has been deflowered. Besides, she will not be able to assist you on your climb upward, for she has no name recognition or position in our world. She will only weigh you down. Millicent Robinson, on the other hand, has a stellar lineage.

This matter is closed."

Tears came to William's eyes as he remembered their conversation. How he wanted to slice into his chest and tear out his beating heart, yet he knew he had no remedy once it was done. For lying their mortally bleeding, he would have no outlet to the one woman who could mend it.

He raked his hand through his hair. Worse than that, he had bedded Juliana, for neither could deny their uncontrollable passion and the love that flowed far past the bounds of physical pleasure. Yet, in admitting he'd done so and found her to be as pure as snow, he condemned her even more to ever being accepted by his family.

There was no way he could win. And now, he'd betrayed both Juliana and Millicent by not being totally honest with either. Perhaps he would be better off dead. Juliana's small home loomed in the distance, swimming before his eyes. For now, he simply wished to die after seeing her.

Minutes later, he was there, and she opened the door, a brilliant smile on her face as she ran out to meet him when he dismounted. Throwing her arms around his neck she kissed him on his lips. He deepened the kiss as he inhaled her essence. She was like an elixir to his tired body. He broke the kiss, his mouth hovering just above her mouth. "Julie, I have longed for you."

"Oh, William." She caressed the side of his face. "I thought I'd go crazy for the sight of you again. Come, let us go inside where wandering eyes and ears cannot intrude."

"Let me put Clancy away."

She sighed. "I suppose the horse deserves some feed and water, though I envy him now."

"It will only be a minute."

Minutes later, he entered the cottage. It smelled, as always, of lemon and fresh air. Today there was also the aroma of fresh baked bread in the air. "You expected me?" he asked.

She grinned. "Fortunate timing. I baked a loaf for here and one for Old Man Higgins up the road. His bones have been aching. I thought this would make him feel better along with some homemade soup."

"You are what will make him well." He exhaled. "Just the sight of you heals."

"I think my food does more."

He strode forward. "You do it for me." His hands roamed over her body.

She grabbed them in hers. "There is time. Please, sit. I want to hear the news. Has your father agreed to our marriage yet?"

His heart sank into his feet. "I wasn't planning on

discussing that right now." He couldn't meet her eyes.

"He hasn't."

William didn't need to see her face to hear the utter disappointment in her voice. "No. there is more." He sank down on to her simple sofa.

Juliana sat next to him. "There is never a need to be concerned about me when telling me the truth, William. Just say it and then I shall deal with it in the best manner I can."

His eyes settled on one point in the floor, at a slightly warped board, just like he was, not quite a fit. "Father insisted I marry another."

Her intake of air was audible. "You are betrothed?"

His hands recoiled into tight balls. "It's worse, Juliana." This time he looked her in the eyes. It was only fair. He saw the reddened rims and unshed tears. He had already injured her deeply. "I married a woman yesterday."

A sob escaped her lips. She clamped her mouth shut as she tightly grabbed the sides of her dress. "I see. And you have consummated the marriage?"

He looked away, too ashamed to say it while still staring at her. "I told her we would have an arrangement. We would have no need to sleep together or have an intimate affair. It was but a suitable business deal, where each had free will to conduct his or her own daily activities—within reason."

She nodded. "Meaning she was to have household responsibilities and you could do as you wished."

He blew out a deep breath. "I did not ask her to perform any chores. Only act as she should in polite circles, go to events. Act the part for those with whom I do business."

"But you could do as you wish."

He stared at her. "You make me sound like a selfish monster."

She nodded. "You have hurt her. You have hurt me. Yet you feel you have the right to have us both on your terms."

"No!" His voice cracked. "I don't want her at all. I want you. I always have."

"You married her." her words were low and almost inaudible. Juliana folded her hands in her lap. "I cannot see a married man. I love you and will never love a man as I love you, but you have asked me to do the impossible."

"But Julie!"

She shook her head. "No, it is as it should be considering your actions. You do not have to tell me, for there is no doubt you have bedded her. The guilt is all over your face. You have given your word to God. Your body has given itself to her. There is nothing left for me but memories of what I wished for but will never be."

"I rode four hours to get here. I am so in need of your

29

warmth."

She stood. "There is no warmth right now for you to share. There is bread and soup. There is a bed to rest in so you can travel home safely and Clancy can feed and rest also. I shall go up the road and deliver my bread and then to a neighbor's and visit, even spend the eve. When I return, you shall be asleep and not bother me. Tomorrow you return to her. You have made your place. You must now live with what you have done."

Chapter Four

Millicent sat behind William's desk and studied his ledger, while Rutherford Lambert, an extremely nervous and spastic accountant, paced about the floor. "This is highly irregular, Mrs. Davis. Mr. Davis is very guarded with whom he shares his business information."

She smiled, yet narrowed her eyes at him, giving the gangly man a clear indication she planned to be civil, yet would take no censure from a hired associate. "Mr. Lambert, William is my husband, not a mere acquaintance or a competitor. It is not likely he would have entered into a union with a person in whom he does not have total trust. And I, likewise, feel the same towards him." *As far as you will ever know.* "I have his best interests at heart, always." *As long as they are also mine.*

He fingered the brim of his hat, the one he'd refused

to set down since he entered with the financial data. "Still, Mrs. Davis, women never…" He paused as he saw what she knew to be her caustic glare. "That is, rarely, do women have access…" Once again, he hesitated, obviously in search of a proper and non-inflammatory word. With a blustery exhale, he resumed his wind and plummeted forward. "It is, in my experience, a rare occurrence for the lady of the house, to desire any input into financial dealings."

"Yes, that's me, rare. So it has been said on numerous occasions." Her eyes continued to peruse the figures and stopped, puzzled at a section on the page. She looked up and laced her fingers together. "You see, I have always had a mind for numbers, strictly from a dollars and cents perspective, mind you. Just never cared for economic forecasts and trends which so often tend to be poppycock. I'm sure you agree that money is a commodity that is precious and should be monitored if one is not to fall prey to those who wish to steal it. I'm certain you feel the same as I, do you not?"

His hat was getting the kneading of its life. "Of course, Madam. Absolutely."

"Splendid." She pushed the ledger across the desk at him. "Then I know you will want to research the discrepancies I found right here. Neither of us would want William to return and find them, would we? I wouldn't at all be surprised if he were to assume, falsely no doubt, that you had purposely absconded with a portion of his funds."

The man's eyes widened into saucers. "Oh, no, Mrs. Davis. Of course not."

She smiled. "Then I suggest you discover where those funds went. If they somehow ended up in another account, I know I can trust you to ensure they return to their proper locations, say, by tomorrow? It is your integrity and profession we're protecting here, isn't it? Not just our money."

He nodded. "Of course, Mrs. Davis. I'll remedy that immediately. I am positive it is only a math error."

"Of course."

He grabbed the ledger and bustled quickly from the office.

Millicent shook her head. There were so many thieves around the wealthy, and few were ever caught. This was the third instance of someone taking advantage of him. The man was far too trustworthy. With regard to this situation, she must be off immediately to the bank to instruct Mr. Etheridge how it should be handled.

Mr. Etheridge would take care of it. She'd simply tell him William had asked that Mr. Lambert have restricted access to all accounts until further notice. Simply put, Lambert could deposit but not withdraw funds. She stood and walked to the door. But first, she had to ask William's personal assistant to arrange immediately for an investigator to follow Mr. Lambert and make sure any funds taken were truly returned. If not, well… She sighed. That was the thing about business. It imitated life. No matter what it threw at you, you did what you had to do.

***

William had dawdled in the city long enough. After spending several days meeting with a number of landlords who attended to his commercial real estate, he was forced to return to his estate and face the woman he'd defiled. Juliana's words still rang in his ears like the sound of a horse drawn hearse. If words had been difficult with his love, he knew they would be harder to draw from his lips once facing Millicent. The woman was mercurial, her moods and actions changing quickly, as if interacting cold and hot fronts blew over moment to moment.

He stabled his horse on his estate and strode to the main house, still considering his words. As he did, his carriage pulled up and once the driver dismounted and opened the door, William realized it was Millicent disembarking. She was dressed impeccably in a gray day dress with black and white trim, her red hair pulled up in back with combs securing it. Gloves already off and in one hand, she stepped out daintily, taking the groom's hand and started toward the home when she saw him and stopped.

A play of conflicting emotion played out over her face. He noted the frown and straightened shoulders, followed by sag of despair, and then finally settling on a forced smile as she ran towards him. "William, you are home already." She threw herself into his arms. "I plan to appear as eager to see you as always," she whispered in his ear. "We shall talk about how I really feel later."

"Darling, I couldn't stay away." He hugged her to him, a nauseous wave crossing over him. "Let us go inside so we can discuss what has happened in my absence." As he stepped back, he saw her eyebrows arch.

"Whatever do you mean?" she asked.

"We can start with what required you travel from home." He smiled as he placed his hand on her back and propelled her towards the front door.

"Oh, William, you know how it is. A new wife simply has to go shopping. There are so many things she'd like to alter to fit her tastes and better the home for both of us and children, perhaps, one day."

His gut twisted. "We have plenty of time to discuss expanding our family. Slow and easy." He nodded as they entered towards his study. "Let us adjourn to my room and sit. I'm sure you have many items which require my ear."

Once inside the closed door, they faced off as obvious adversaries. Her face contorted with anger. "How dare you ask me where I have been? You, yourself, were not where you said you would be. I checked."

He grabbed her by the arm and nearly dragged her to a chair. "Sit down. Now."

"I will not be ordered."

He pushed her into it. "Stay there and listen. I am the man and you are the woman. No matter how much you'd like to grow an appendage, you are without one. In this society, the man rules. Though you may wish it were not so, I have the power and you shall follow my lead. Life will go much more smoothly if you follow convention."

She crossed her arms, her color rising to a deep red. "Before you demean me so, I believe it is in your best interest to listen and not continue to blather on. I have saved you a great deal of money in your absence."

He paced in front of her, his hands clasped behind him. "Pray continue." The woman could be provoking but was smart. He knew better than to discount her statement as immaterial.

"I discovered a discrepancy in your books. A rather large amount of money was missing from your accounts."

He turned, placing his hands on his hips. "How dare you review my finances?"

"I am your wife, William." She played with her gloves. "You said yourself that I had a brilliant business mind. I can read figures and understand accounting on much of a simple level. It takes no genius. Of course it is always nice to be able to depend on hired specialists to do the right thing and perform the job given. Still, there are times when that does not occur. In this case it did not."

He nodded. "You know this how?"

She smiled. "According to Mr. Etheridge at the bank, the funds in question were withdrawn by Mr. Lambert in small amounts over a rather long period. There is no accounting for where these funds went. Mr. Etheridge said that considering the length of time in which these funds had been withdrawn, there probably was very little chance they could be found and replaced."

He nodded, nerves stretched to the point of popping. His face burned and gut seized. "What did Mr. Lambert say about the missing funds?"

She sighed. "That's just it. I simply informed him he needed to correct the record, never once inferring I believed him to be less than honest. He never had a chance to report back. It seems the man met with a very unfortunate accident. Set upon by thieves in the city. The man was found in the alley with three bullets to the head."

***

William had never been much of a drinker. However, the current situation drove him, yet again, to the bottle. Though this time there would be no repeat of the spectacle he had made of himself just a few nights ago. No, this time he would ensure he had peace by sleeping here in his study. To hell with Millicent interrupting his agony.

Rutherford Lambert, God rest his soul. Dead in an alley. Shot. If William didn't know better, he'd swear the man took his own life. He doubted any person could shoot himself that many times in the middle of the forehead. Yet the man's death was an odd twist of irony that had saved William's hide from being further exposed by his sleuth of a wife.

How was he now supposed to send Juliana funds? Though his love was provoked with him at this time and standing steadfast to her morals, as she rightfully should, a trait which he had always admired, he would not let the woman die of poverty with such a meager income as her sewing would allow.

He exhaled sharply. Rutherford had been opposed to hiding the funds in William's personal finances. William had told him he'd prefer no trace of their disbursement. "After all," he'd told his accountant, "these are my personal accounts, not those of any business enterprise. Who is to know?"

Who indeed? A snoop of a wench who had to have her nose up his arse. Now Rutherford had died. Tragically. Leaving William with burgeoning guilt and not a thought as to how he would transfer monies so Millicent was none the wiser. He'd think of an answer. William took a swig from his glass. The Bourbon flowed down his throat like liquid fire. No Scotch tonight, not that this was any better. Still, it had clouded his mind already, and if he knew nothing, he knew no serious decisions should be made while imbibing. *Why didn't you remember that before you ravished Millicent you imbecile?*

He tapped the side of his glass on his chin and pondered. "Why was she not angrier at him for his indiscretion? It had been his failure to tell the truth about his whereabouts that she'd attacked when first seeing him. Then she had launched into finances. She was indeed unpredictable.

Setting down his glass, he leaned back in his chair. Perhaps despite her discomfort she had enjoyed their session. Most interesting. The first amusing thought of the evening crossed his mind. *Perhaps she wishes for me to repeat our tryst.* Not on her life. Though her body was toned and breasts high, he would die alone and celibate before he touched her.

Unless he was desperate.

He reached for the glass and took another sip. Surely, better his wife than a common lady of the night. But not now. Not anytime soon. He had not yet ruled out winning Juliana back as his.

***

Millicent sat up in bed and punched her pillow. Try as

39

she would, she could not sleep. William was not in bed, for she certainly would have heard him. She should not care after their last encounter, but surprisingly, she did. Her body throbbed for more than just a kiss. She had now convinced herself that her mother had been correct in saying once she was entered for the first time it could then be pleasurable. However, it seemed William was bent on making sure that it did not have a chance of reoccurring.

She threw her legs out over the bed. How was she supposed to live an entire lifetime with no man to fondle her, no one to drive her into the throes of passion she had read about in her books? So many would not have been written if such a furor had been obtained by many. She knew without contemplation it could happen to her.

I must find William. Her mind made up, she stood and grabbed a robe from the bottom of the bed. With care, she could avoid the servants. Surely most, if not all, had retired. Stealthily slipping downstairs, she padded across to William's study. Most likely he was cowering inside, afraid his baser instincts would emerge like a roaring lion. It was that thought that drove her on.

After a tentative knock and no answer, she opened the door, to see him laid out on the sofa, his cravat removed, shirt and pants off. He was already covered with a small coverlet, no doubt kept downstairs for nights as this.

Closing the door and locking it, she tiptoed to the

sofa. There, she discarded her robe and nightshirt before removing William's covering and unceremoniously climbing up on him. He didn't budge.

Pooh, this is not good. I need relief. I need to be fondled and entered. She grasped his cock in her hand and began to slide down his length. It immediately responded to her stroking. As she continued her magic, William stirred. He reached out, his eyes still closed. "Julie."

Momentarily she froze. Who the hell was Julie? Tossing that in the back of her mind for later, she concentrated on the here and now. Damn the man. He was going to have sex. His cock was becoming engorged. As it filled and stood of its own accord, his eyes still shut, she took the liberty of mounting him. Sliding onto his shaft she shivered. Her mother was correct. No pain. She rose up and slid down again, convulsing as small tentacles of sensation coursed through her.

As if on cue, William surged up into her and began to move beneath her, groaning. She met his thrusts by moving downward, sensation beginning to build in her core. Oh, my God, it was glorious. Why would not every woman want to be on top? For the bulk of him remained inside with every movement.

He groaned and pumped harder.

She panted and moved more rapidly.

They surged together, faster and faster. Her world

41

tilted as spirals of heat wavered inside, engulfing her as they swept over, burning her skin. She surged down quickly as he met her. As she reached a place where she never thought to climb, shaking and wanting to hold on to the overwhelming joy of the moment, he moved sideways.

"What the bloody hell!"

William toppled her off him as he slid out from his spot. "My God, woman, what do you think you're doing?"

She got to her feet shaking, her ire building in sizzling irritation. He had just ruined her pinnacle. "I would think that would speak for itself."

"You had no right."

She gasped and then began to laugh first from embarrassment, then to relieve tension. "To hell I don't. Who made you the poor violated weakling? I have every right as a wife to be pleasured as much as you. Or has someone assumed that role for me?"

He looked at the floor. "I have been drinking, Millicent. I did not know what I was doing."

She grabbed her robe and threw it on. "For a man who wasn't aware of his actions, your cock was wide awake."

"Men often wake up with an erection. Not thrusting with any willful intention inside a woman."

Trying with great difficulty to control her emotions, Millicent took a deep breath. "Who is Julie?"

His eyes widened, as he licked his lips and looked away. "I…I suppose it was the maid at my host's house while I was in town."

She scowled. "You are a terrible liar. If you don't want me, never mind. I will not impose myself on you again. But head my warning. Let me find out you've touched that woman once and I will ruin you. As for her, you don't even want to know."

Chapter Five

Millicent scowled as she had her breakfast. He'd taken off again, but this time in earnest for a business meeting in the city. At least this time, he'd had the courtesy to tell her as she walked to the breakfast table. Grabbing a croissant, she broke it as she would have liked to break his neck. How many times would she put up with a man leaving her when she was not totally fulfilled? He was fortunate he had plenty of money or he'd meet his demise today. The man missed his mark by not being born female. Last night his simpering protests of being debased made her want to vomit.

Never more would she seek sex from him or even desire it. He was too weak. If he could venture off in search of illicit partners, then so could she. The difference was she knew how to pick and dispose of them so they would never breathe a word. When Millicent was only seven, her mother had demonstrated how to do it for her. But far different from her mother, she would never be in the position of actually pulling the trigger. Finding people one could pay to do that was all too easy if one had the money at one's disposal to do so.

She chuckled. William couldn't hide anything if his life depended on it. But she could. She had only to purchase a trifle and then return it, unbeknownst to him. Once she pocketed the currency, she would pay the right person to eliminate the one who vexed her. Still one individual was never enough to have at your immediate call. Best to have a loyal man and a back-up waiting in the wings. She had such a man in Robert, whom she'd found through fortunate circumstances in town. A rogue and former employee of her stepfather's who was only too willing to eliminate obstacles to her happiness. For a price. She'd introduced him to the staff as a *runner* and he was. He ran when she ordered. It would only take a short while before she identified another likely candidate. But for now, on to seeking a suitable outlet for her passion. Afterwards, alas, all good things would come to an end, for each one she selected would expire from the most terrible tragedy. Yet some would have longer lives than others, dependent on how well each was able to bring her to release and had followed the rules.

She must choose the first man. Not just a loyal subject

who could care less about his dominance, but one who could ease the ache between her legs.

In the meantime she would send Robert on a search to discover just who Julie might be. For to find her and rid William of his obsession would do her a world of good. "Then how will you feel about me?" she murmured. Things would change for the better, she was sure of it.

She leaned back and crossed her legs. Now, who would be the best candidates for her toy? She was thinking athletic, young, not too bright, and oh so willing to give up cock and morals to satisfy her. Her fantasies got the better of her as she envisioned a muscular, strapping male licking her in her most sensitive spot. That would put a man where he really belonged. Most importantly, he must be someone who knew when to keep his mouth to himself. Unless she desired it. She thought she'd start with the stable.

Still salivating over her decision early next morning, Millicent donned her riding habit prepared to call for a stable boy to ready a suitable mount. Little did he know he possibly could be it. But first, the criteria. Strong, strapping and hung. He also had to have tight lips and, if need be, become Robert's backup with the ability to kill at will without remorse. It was a difficult order.

Approaching the entryway, the main groomsman met her. "Madam, allow me to choose a horse for you."

She eyed him up and down, noticing for the first time his attributes. A bit older than she had in mind, but well-toned and handsome. Perhaps only a sprinkling of years her senior. "Harrison, I fancy a high spirited stallion with a zest for adventure."

His eyes widened. "One of our horses, Madam? Did you have one in mind?"

She grinned, linking her arm with his. "Oh yes, Harrison. Let us discuss it in your office."

***

William sat on his mount and rubbed his eyes as he rode. A month had gone by since last he saw Juliana. They had never gone that long between assignations. No note had come from her, though he had sent money, cash from a business transaction which he asked his business partner to book as personal expenses. Apparently, she'd decided to stay firm in not seeing him now that he was married.

Millicent had not bothered him either, seeming extremely chipper for a woman who believed she'd been scorned. It suited him. She was clever with household business matters, so as long as she stayed out of his personal matters, he would not in any way disturb their arrangement. Still he believed he needed to explain to Juliana that his marriage was a sham. Perhaps she would reconsider seeing him. He ached for her. She had to capitulate.

With that thought on his mind, he rode down the hill towards her cottage in the distance. It was his dearest wish that she would greet him as she had when last he came. As he neared, there was no sign of Juliana. He made it to the front door and tied up the horse there for the moment. Here was hoping he wouldn't have to mount again in a few moments. As he started to knock at the door it swung open, and she rushed into his arms.

"William, oh my sweet dear. I have hated how we last parted."

He pulled her so close to him, for a moment he was afraid he'd crushed the air from her. The fragrance of her hair wafted around him. He inhaled it as if it were pure oxygen. Then leaning down, he kissed her, first gently, then absorbing her into him, afraid he would never again have the chance.

She responded in kind, her hands roaming across his back. It was she who finally broke their embrace, out of breath and flushed. "I cannot live without you, darling. I have told myself it is wrong, yet every moment without you is like the sentence of sure death. Please tell me you still love me as much. Or, have you found that your affection for your wife is more than you previously thought?"

"I will always love only you." He drew his hands down her side, lingering over her full bust. It appeared even larger than before. "As for Millicent, she has become not only an obstacle but a thorn in my side. For now, she leaves me alone and I pray it continues. Juliana, I will never have intimate relations with her again. In my mind I am divorced from the woman."

She took a deep breath. "But in the mind of the court and of society, you are not. I can never be seen as your true wife until Millicent is gone."

He nodded. "I understand, but at this time I can do nothing about it. Perhaps once my father is deceased, I can move on and make the arrangements I wish for."

"Still tied to your father's bank account?"

He shuffled his feet. "I would not have the position I do now without his backing. I would be of no use to you as a pauper."

Her eyes were wet with tears. "I suppose you are correct. I doubt you could ever assume my simple style of living. Pray come inside. I have news. Leave Clancy where he is this time."

William followed her into the cottage and immediately inhaled the familiar scent lemon as well as the aroma of a pot of beans cooking on the wood stove. "Your home always smells like love."

"It is my oasis from life's trials." She sat on the sofa and patted the cushion next to her.

He obediently joined her, clasping her hands. "What is

it you need to tell me."

Her color rose and her neck splotched in a deep red. "After you left last time, I had quite a bout of sickness. It went on every morning for more than a week, and I feared I had been poisoned by something I ate. I bartered with the village doctor for an examination." Her chest heaved. "William, I am with child."

Sparks flew down his limbs. Carried away on a wave of conflicting emotions, he momentarily thought he would faint dead away. He squeezed her hands, a great joy flushing him. "Julie, a child? Ours?"

She nodded. "Of course, ours. I have been with no other man nor could I ever bear to be."

"Is the baby…all right?"

Smiling, she rubbed his thumb. The doctor says he is fine. Of course, there is no way to scientifically determine his gender, but I know it is a boy. He will have your brown hair and blue eyes."

"His eyes could be gold."

She shook her head. "They could be but they're not. I know this."

"You must let me set you up in town where you will be safe."

"No." She said it as if there no use arguing. "I have said this home is my oasis and so it is. I will stay and our son will be safe here. On this I am firm."

***

"You found her? Where?" A surge of excitement consumed Millicent as she stared up into Robert's face.

"In the country, about a four-hour ride from here. I had Farley follow Mr. Davis to her cottage."

Anger swiftly replaced her excitement. "He went to see her?"

He nodded. "And spent the night. They kissed at the door as he left."

She stood and strode about the room in an effort to keep from exploding. "I see. Did Farley happen to overhear anything?"

"Of course." Robert looked away from her. "I told you I chose him well to help me. The man is loyal and a good spy. He slept in the basement, entering by the stairs on the side of the house. At daybreak, he went outside and waited until Mr. Davis emerged."

"Hurry up. Out with it, what was said?"

The man swallowed hard. "Mr. Davis told her to take care of their son and patted her stomach."

"She's pregnant?" Millicent winced at the sound of her shriek. Turning away from Robert she squeezed her hands together and gulped for air. Slowly concentrating on calm she did not feel, she turned. "I apologize, but this comes as a shock."

"I understand."

"Have my horse readied. Since Harrison was so sadly trampled in the barn, I suppose you must help some poor stable boy in readying the stead."

He nodded. "So I shall. Madam, should I recruit more men for the stable? I fear we may be short-staffed in due time."

She chuckled. "Robert you are such a dear to consider my needs. For now let us go attend to tying up loose ends."

Later that afternoon she, attended by Robert and Farley, arrived at Juliana's cottage. "Small and rustic, don't you think?"

He nodded. "Yes, Madam."

She sighed. "No matter. This will take only a few minutes. Wait for me next to the barn." She dismounted and stepped up on the porch. Before she could knock, the door opened. A woman with long flowing brown hair and striking eyes stared at her, the woman's cheeks stained scarlet. "You're Millicent, aren't you?"

Millicent smiled, wanting to scratch out her eyes, not act civil. However the former would not garner the final result she wished for. "You are correct. William has told me of your pregnancy and I am here to see to it that his wishes are met and you are cared for appropriately."

Juliana's eyes narrowed and her eyes spoke their meaning. "William would never have told you. Why are you really here?"

Millicent shrugged as she barged her way into Juliana's home. "Think what you wish, dear, the matter remains the same. You are a hindrance to his position and livelihood. I am thus forced, in his best interests, to intervene. You carry his child and only potential heir. *For now.*" Emphasizing the last two words, she paused and studied the woman. It was no wonder she had attracted him, but she would attract no more. "I must ensure your safety. However, that does not mean I need to sit idly by and watch you make a mockery of my vows and continue to cavort with my husband."

A sob escaped Juliana's lips. "What do you wish me to do? I cannot help how I feel."

"So that may be." Millicent strode around the room, fingering the quilt on the sofa. "That does not negate the fact you are a threat to William and his future as long as you are in contact with him and close to his estate."

"But, I am four hours away."

Millicent resisted the urge to grab the woman and throttle her. "Only a day's ride. As you can see, I am here and it is not that late. You must leave here and find quarters where William does not communicate with you except for notes which Farley or Robert will deliver on your behalf. I will make sure you have funds. But, whatever you do, do not be foolish enough to write anything in your messages that will in any way connect me to this or denigrate me."

Tears poured down Juliana's face. "I suppose I should have known this would happen. I will agree to your terms for the baby comes first. I am a woman of integrity and will not cross you."

Millicent smiled. "Fine. Feel free to write a note and Farley shall stay behind to help you pack."

Juliana gasped. "Now? This minute?"

"Of course. Once the note reaches William, you must be long gone."

A half hour later, as Millicent and Robert left Juliana's property, he turned to her. "Mrs. Davis, are you sure keeping the wench alive is a good idea? As of now, she is carrying his only heir. I can easily dispose of her with no one the wiser."

She glanced at Robert and smiled. He had proven to be a valuable and discreet asset. "No, I intend to keep her alive, *and* her bastard if necessary. She may be needed for a trump card later. Time will tell if that will be necessary."

***

William sat on the sofa in his office, alone with his misery. The note from Juliana was tucked away safely in his vest pocket. Tears escaped his eyes despite his attempt to restrain them. She'd said she would never leave her home. She had been as a sentinel about that desire. Yet only days afterwards she had left and there was no way to track her. How could she do it so calmly when she claimed to love him so much? Her only statement was for him not to worry and that, when the time was right, she would send his son to him for schooling and preparation for the position which he eventually would assume.

He sobbed into his fist. Millicent had been poised about the matter, only saying Juliana had visited her on leaving her cottage and asked she deliver the note. According to Millicent, she'd promised to have Robert keep in touch with Juliana, but she had promised Juliana she nor William would ever know where Julie was. It was her agreement with his love. "I will, of course send money with Robert," she'd told him. "Never would I let the mother of your child suffer, no matter how I feel about your relationship."

He had no alternative but to accept her statement on face value, though his gut told him there was something left unsaid. How could he ever live without his Juliana? It was like living in total darkness, a void of nothingness. He could only hold to the one ray of hope that shone within this whole sordid mess. His son would come to live with him.

1889, New York City

"Dead, are you sure?" William's words came out barely louder than a whisper. His head hung in defeat.

Millicent nodded. The time had come to play the trump. Only two days ago he had told her they should consider separation, and that would never be. She enjoyed having the power she had now. "Completely sure, William. I sent Robert to her as always. It seems Juliana was ill, consumption. Her son died at her side of the same awful disease." Millicent marveled at how well she played the part of the sympathetic wife.

Her nails dug into the lounge. A remarkable performance really, in spite of the fact his mistress and bastard were involved.

"I can't say that I'm dreadfully sorry, William, but you did deserve to know what became of them. I was determined to help, have always been so as you know, despite your lack of admiration for my efforts. Now you know."

William nodded. "So I do." He raised his head, allowing her to see the red rims of his eyes, the batting of his dark lashes fighting back unshed tears. "Millicent, I know I haven't been a very good husband. I should never have suggested we separate. That was said in a moment of anger and loneliness. It is time for me to cast that aside. You've been right all along, and I have been selfish. I should never have hesitated starting a family, instead of foolishly wishing that Caleb, despite his circumstances, could come live with us." He placed his hand on hers. "We will have a son."

"Of course we will." Miranda smiled. Victory was sweet. *All it took was one small murder and the quiet disposal of your past.*

Not the End, but the Beginning

This story now ends, but this is really the beginning. Millicent and William live on, and with their money, they can prolong their lives. William's son, Caleb, a son whom William believes to be dead, survives by a quirk of fate. Now grown and joined by the woman Caleb intends to marry, Caleb and Winnifred are suspended in time. All four late nineteenth/ twentieth century aristocrats survive to live another life in yet another century, in a very different United States, with Millicent and William at the helm. Or is there only one who rules?

FROZEN ASSETS

Chapter One

Caleb Cash stared upward, panic seizing him as the huge blob of frozen matter exploded. Swirling crystals showered down. Icicles stabbed the snow, gouging the earth, piercing it like daggers. Blinding snow raged. Stinging needles slashed the army-issued blanket with a relentless rain of spikes. Pulling his coat off, he threw it over his head. Ablaze, a bright green light flashed, its blast rocketing it toward the cave. The red hot ball of flaming ash surged from the sky, prepared to claim the landscape. He turned and ran inside the cave. Sizzling heat crackled in his ears, and exploded through the opening, bent on destruction.

Snow pellets, then sub-zero water flooded the hole, hurling him backwards. Caleb grasped his throat, unable to breathe. Launched helplessly through the air, he grabbed at the ice-filled void as darkness captured him in its glacial, icy fingers. Fire and ice, an atomic mixture of hopelessness. Clenching him, claiming him, for all eternity.

Caleb struggled as his frigid body groped against the solid case of his prison. Shaking like a man too long for a drink, he clawed at the crystalline interior, his movement impaired, his nerves tingling with sharp jabs against otherwise unfeeling tissue. Winnifred, where was she? Complete consciousness evaded him. But his mind. His mind recorded everything.

***

"Tem-pera-ture rea-ching nine-ty-one degrees."

Doctor Fran Victor turned to Nicky, Andro Model 6052 circa 2138 to the techs, and chuckled. "What's with the antiquated speech?"

Nicky grinned. "I watched an old sci-fi vid from the nineteen-eighties last night on the hologramic interphase. They had things called robots. Hunks of tin." He snickered. "I am a vast improvement, don't you think?"

"Indeed." She smiled. Tall and with his dark blond hair and blue eyes, Nicky passed for human as long as he wasn't wearing the black Andro uniform. "I, for one, think you should have been programmed with emotions."

He cocked his head and gazed at her, his look thoughtful. Fran would never get over it. As an Andro, he was considered a machine to use and discard. But he was more. He was smart, funny, and she'd swear she saw his soul when looking deeply into those azure eyes.

"I have humor, thanks to my tech. What else should I want?"

"Never mind. If I elaborated, you wouldn't get my point."

"If you are speaking of the act of human copulation, you are correct." He bowed his head. "It appears to be uncomfortable and most embarrassing. Who would want to spread body fluids over each other?" He seemed to shake his head in pity as he looked at her through twinkling eyes.

Too bad. While Nicky wasn't programmed to act on it, his model was fully equipped to satisfy a woman and his memory banks held the history of sexual techniques. Sighing, she nodded. "Like I said, you wouldn't get it. Don't worry, it isn't important. And since you're assigned to me and I never get any, you'll never be exposed to my, um, discomfort."

"How are the two early twentieth-century humans?"

At Doctor Brock Green's voice, Fran turned and watched him saunter into the lab, wearing mustard-colored scrubs. She frowned. How could anyone look good in that color? Yet, he did. Tall and thin, black hair, large soulful brown eyes and lashes women spent a fortune to emulate. Too bad his looks were a lie and his sour business-only attitude was the truth.

"Amazingly well. Of course, how they got in that state is the big question. We're still analyzing the green dust covering them." She jerked her head toward the electron microscope hooked to banks of computers. "So far, nothing. I hope the procedure used on them in the nineteen-forties hasn't put them at greater risk than whatever happened originally."

"Shouldn't be a problem. The Primera and her husband were cryoed at the same time." He stared through the one-way glass.

"If I'm correct about the substance covering them, we may finally have a method to put a person in stasis without freezing." She frowned. "As for what happened in the nineteen-forties, from what I've learned the order came from the top of the food chain."

"Interesting." Arms folded across his chest, he tapped his lips with his stylus. "Just the beginning of the takeover of free-will."

She glanced at Nicky and saw his worried expression matched her thoughts. "You'd better watch what you say or the Police for Peace will send you down to Antarctica."

With a snort, he stared down his nose at them. "The damned POPs are too busy smoking weed and palming money. Don't get me started."

Fran exhaled low and soft. Something had gotten Doctor Brock Green's attention. And for it to break through his science-only mind, it was cataclysmic, earth shattering, life-altering. "What's happened?"

He looked at her, his mouth still in a thin grim line. "Don't you ever watch the news?"

Interesting. Once again he'd broken pattern. When did he ever watch anything other than telecast scientific conferences? For that matter, when did he start watching the news? "Not really. I rely on Nicky for a recap."

Nicky nodded. "Morning news. Regime terrorists strike again, destroying government facility in Atlanta. Ten terrorists in custody, awaiting transfer to maximum security, Antarctica."

"To die an unnatural death of hypothermia and bodies burned in ovens that operate twenty-four/seven," Brock added.

"You're so full of shit!" Fran checked the control on the humans. Almost ninety-three. "They may be in prison, but they live inside a pressurized climate-control bubble."

He slanted her a glance. "Have you ever been down there or seen the facility using satellite?"

"Well no, but—"

"I got an eyeful before the government discovered that eye-in-the-sky was still operational and accessible by the public. People are stripped and thrown outside in pens. Once dead, the evidence is burned." He growled under his breath, sounding more animal than human.

"You sound like a Regime Terrorist."

"Fran, get with it. The terrorists are freedom fighters. People like you and me who want to be out from government control. Not observed through microchips, told where they'll work and what work they're allowed to do based on some computer spitting out what's needed."

"Sounds like you've been going to their secret rallies."

He shook his head. "Maybe I was given too much education and now I want to think for myself."

"What the hell?" the female screamed from the covered examination tube. She struggled to sit up from the table. "Blast you, Caleb Cash, now you've gone and abducted me."

***

Winnifred scanned the sterile-looking pale green walls of her prison. No windows and a locked door meant no escape. The smell of alcohol and chemicals plus the scientific equipment overwhelmed and terrified her. The few oddly misshapen chairs didn't look to offer comfort. But what held her attention was a small, flashy gadget with knob and controls, about the size of a motion picture projector that sat on a long table next to her.

She eyed the man and woman and the odd assistant in the strange one-piece black suit as they entered her room. Except for missing antennae, they looked like the moon people off the cover of *Amazing Stories*.

"Am I an experiment? Are you from the moon? Have you traveled far though the Milky Way?"

The woman laughed. "Hell no. There's nothing up on the moon but craters. They couldn't even make the settlement work. Look, let's take this slow. We'll tell you what we know and you can share."

"Spies." Winnifred nodded. "I should have known. The war is over, but my father warned the Germans would gear-up to retake what they lost. I am an experiment, aren't I? Are you testing some kind of chemical warfare? And where is Caleb? Have you killed him? Are you going to kill me?"

"Stop talking," ordered a harsh voice.

Her gaze flew from the dark-haired woman and blond-haired man to a man in an ugly mustard two-piece suit.

"If you'll be quiet, we can try to fill in the blanks."

She blinked. "Fill in the blanks?"

"Tell you what we know, answer your questions." The petite woman pulled one of the hard chairs over and sat facing her. "I'm Doctor Fran Victor, the creep looking like someone vomited all over him is Doctor Brock Green and the blond in black is Nicky. He's an Andro."

Winnifred's eyes narrowed. "Andro?" Her gaze slid to the strange blue-eyed man in black. Something about him wasn't quite right. He looked normal, almost, but in her gut she knew he wasn't.

Doctor Victor's gaze flitted to Nicky then back to her. "Android, part machine, part human and very intelligent. He's also my best friend."

Winnifred swallowed hard. "Your best friend is an automaton?" Where was she that such a thing could happen?

"Yes, and he's the most loyal being you will ever meet."

Nicky cleared his throat. "I am molecularly assembled as a combination of the best of manpower and knowledge known on Earth and all the surrounding planets, with the features of the best computers known as of the year 2,138. I am *Good Housekeeping* approved, Government-certified and an award-winning Andro of the future. None of my brothers or I have ever had a failure, glitch, bug." He batted his eyelashes. "I am also very loveable."

"If you're really part machine, I would hope you don't have a glitch or bug." Winnifred couldn't take her eyes off him. He looked real, the kind of man in the pictures that women swooned over. She chortled. "This is either a joke or I'm asleep dreaming, reliving one of the stories I love."

One look at the somber faces staring at her said she really was in 2138. But on the off chance she was wrong, "Or not. Is this a joke of Cash's? Because if it is, it isn't working. I read *Amazing Stories*. This looks nothing like future." She scanned the room, then focused on the serious faces before her. "It can't be 2,138."

"You're right, it isn't. It's 2141. And *Cash* isn't in any shape to play a joke on anyone at the moment." Doctor Brock Green crossed his arms. "He hasn't awakened yet."

"What do you mean hasn't awakened?" Winnifred looked around and saw the long cylinder tube next to the one she had climbed out of. "Is Caleb in there?"

Brock nodded. "He's fine. For now concentrate on my questions. When and what's the last thing you remember?"

"November 11, 1918. A roar, like thunder. Caleb running and me following, searing heat and then ice pelting me."

"The two of you have been in stasis, suspended animation for two hundred and twenty-three years." His gaze met hers. "We discovered you when digging out a meteor. We still don't understand why you didn't revive when exposed to fresh air."

"What?" Another tremor of unease rippled through her.

"The only explanation is green dust that was on you from the meteor that sealed you in the cave. In the nineteen forties, you were discovered in a stasis-like condition and were flash frozen in a method we call cryo."

Winnifred twiddled with her fingers, checking to see if she still had full control of her faculties and struggled not to laugh like some hysterical female. She needed to stay calm, apply the reason for which she was famous. The reason that had allowed her to lead the Suffragette movement. The reason she could stand firm against the male tyranny of her time. It was the only way she could decipher what Doctor Green just told her. "If I understand correctly, Caleb and I were alive, yet asleep, found and then frozen, pardon me, cryoed, by you for over two-hundred years."

Fran nodded. "Except you were in the cave for twenty-three years and have been frozen for two hundred."

Winnifred ignored the lessening numbness in her fingers and increasing burn as if she'd hit her funny bone. Heart racing like a horse in the last furlong of the Kentucky Derby, she slid off the table and headed toward the open door, her legs wobbling under her like a newborn foal's.

"Sedative!" Doctor Brock ordered as Nicky rushed up to her.

Before she could stop him, Nicky pressed a long, thin cylinder against her hand. Cool, moist pressure hit her skin. Smiling, he held out his arms. "Allow me to break your fall."

"No thank you." Winnifred took one step and collapsed.

***

"I'm not surprised she didn't believe you," Caleb said. "She has a strong suspicion of anyone's motives, even back in nineteen-eighteen. She believed with every fiber I wanted her to be my brood mare." He snorted. "Nothing could have been further from the truth. I wanted her for her name, social position and intelligence." *And under my body with her long legs wrapped around my waist.*

"I'm surprised to see you're taking our explanation about what has transpired so well," Fran said. "This must be like going into the Twilight Zone."

"Twilight Zone?"

"He's too early by forty-one years to know about that." Nicky grinned. "It's a show. I love watching it on the old vids. Although, I am surprised the Primera even allows them. They say so much about us even now."

"What's a vid and The Twilight Zone?"

"Oh, yes, sorry," Nicky said. "A vid is a way of watching shows, even old ones. The Zone premiered in nineteen fifty-nine on American television. It was broadcast for five years. However, upon becoming a cult-favorite it is still watched avidly by fans." He stared at the woman he called Fran. "With each generation breeds passionate new fans."

"Amazing." Caleb turned to Fran. "Is he a walking encyclopedia?"

"And more," Nicky said.

"I could have explained as well." Brock said. He looked at Caleb. "For all his wealth of knowledge, there are many things Nicky doesn't know."

"If you're going to launch into another discussion about human copulation—"

"Nicky!" Fran threw the Andro a stern look.

Caleb smiled. "These half-man machines are fascinating. I think I'll like this world." He sighed as he eased off the table. "Okay, the legs aren't real steady, but if someone will find me a good horse and direct me to a boarding house, I'd like to check out what this new world is like."

Fran looked at him and darted a glance at Brock. "I'm afraid you can't do that."

Eyes narrowed, Caleb's gaze slid between them. "Why not? I thought I wasn't a prisoner. Yes, I've been asleep. But surely I haven't lost my freedom. This is still the United States of America, land of the free, isn't it?"

"Yes, but," Fran paused as she glanced at Brock, "for now it isn't safe for you to go out into society."

"What she hasn't told you, is you can't go out without debriefing and a microchip," Brock snarled.

Caleb's teeth snapped together. He was beginning to dislike this new world. "A microchip?"

Fran stared at him, her face drawn in a bleak frown. "We are scientists. All citizens in our time have a small mechanical disc implanted at the base of the neck, just under the skin. It tracks you at all times."

"Do you mean the government can track where I am and what I do?" His snort turned to laughter. "Surely you jest."

Nicky, Fran and Brock shook their heads.

Caleb leaned forward and rested his hands on the table. "You should have left me frozen."

Chapter Two

Winnifred woke and turned her head to the left at the sound of a cough. Caleb sat there, on a small mattress just across from her. They were no longer in the equipment-filled room but had been moved to a tiny one with an open doorway. "Where am I?"

"Now, now, my dear Winnifred. The question is … where are *we?*" Caleb's tight smile disappeared as his lips thinned. "Next time, tamp down on the temper and they won't drug you. You were knocked out for eight hours. If you'd kept quiet and asked questions you'd have been around to learn we're in a mess."

"Are you blaming my lack of consciousness on weak will? I'm not responsible for a blasted comet hitting us and the ensuing events." She struggled to a sitting position, brushing her hair off her face. Frowning, she realized it was loose, void of all hairpins.

He exhaled sharply. "I wasn't speaking of our unfortunate freezing."

He leaned back against his bed, his arms folded across his chest and ankles crossed. His relaxed posture didn't fool her. She'd met him on a number of occasions and observed him on even more unseen. Even when drawing to an inside straight he'd looked at ease. Right now, she knew he was tighter than an over-wound watch spring. For once his tension showed in his dark chocolate eyes.

"I was speaking of the sedative you got after we awoke in 2,141."

She started to laugh. "They haven't gotten you believing that lie, have they?"

She smothered a smile as he raked his hands through his longish, wavy dark brown hair. Over the months she'd spied on him, she'd envied those fingers their ability to touch that silky mane. He was the only man she'd ever met who at six feet two inches, and a foot taller than her, didn't make her feel insignificant but rather wanted and protected. Maybe that was why he so angered her, he upset all her beliefs. She'd never admit it, but she'd always envied his former wife, Harriet. If one had to die, to do so in the middle of being pleasured seemed the perfect way to pass from this mortal plane.

"Winnifred, it isn't a lie. We're in deep trouble. This isn't the world or the country we knew. If we knew then what would happen, I question whether we'd have fought any of our wars."

"What are you talking about?"

"It means that in this time no one, not even us, your so called more privileged men and women, have the freedom to come and go as we like. We are monitored by an implanted device."

"The hell we are." She pushed off the table and stood. "I don't see any bars or guards. I'm leaving." She took a step. Once again, her legs buckled. Locking her knees, she stiff-leggedly weaved to the open doorway of their small room. Nearing it, she rushed forward and slammed into hard air and fell backward onto the floor.

She heard Caleb sighed, as she lay on there, her face and chest aching from smashing into something that wasn't there. "What happened? Why can't I leave? The blasted door is open."

"Force field."

She struggled into a sitting position. "This is getting old." She licked her lips. Blasted man looked more delectable than an ice on a blistering day in July.

He grinned. "Thank God, you haven't changed your mule-stubborn headstrong ways. By the way, I like that in a woman." His chuckle quickly turned to deep laughter. "Sorry. It feels good to laugh. To be honest, you would have put a star in vaudeville to shame with that pratfall."

Winnifred rolled her eyes. "I'm not going to ask which one. What is a force field?"

He smiled. "According to Doctor Brock Green, it's an invisible barrier erected to prevent someone from entering or leaving a room or enclosure yet giving the illusion you have freedom. We are, more rather than less, prisoners."

"I will be no one's prisoner." She pushed herself off the floor and stood; her legs finally willing to hold her weight. "How do we escape?"

"I suggest, my dear, you sit on the cot they've provided and for once be still." He pointed to her cot against the facing wall with a table standing between the beds. "It's critical you pay attention to what I say. And what they say later. We have to wait until we have assembled sufficient information to determine a means of extricating ourselves from our current dismal condition."

"In other words, shut up and observe."

"I knew you were smart." Caleb grinned, then glanced at the open but secured doorway and growled. "So far, I have learned the two doctors, Fran Victor and Brock Green, hold different positions within the government. I'm unsure what the current administration goals or plans for us are. The only thing I'm confident of is the United State is no longer the land of the free and the government is not of the people, for the people and by the people."

"We weren't before." Winnifred rose and, dusting off

her skirts, ambled to her cot. "It was a government of the men, for the men and by the men. Not that it would have remained that way much longer." Grinning, she collapsed onto the bed, her back resting against the wall and stared across the small space between their beds.

"According to Nicky, the first woman became president in the early twenty-first century. I think he said it was in twenty-twenty. Now it seems women have all the reins."

As his dark looks turned hard, she raised an eyebrow. "How so?"

He frowned. "A woman's in power. She's in charge. A ruthless tyrant."

"What's her name?"

His jaw clenched in a tight grimace and eyes hardened to shard of coal. "Mil Davis, but she's called the Primera."

"Hold on," she said. "Wasn't there a tycoon back before the comet hit us named William Davis, married to a woman nicknamed Mil the Millionaire?"

He nodded. "It appears they were also cryogenically frozen. Although her revival was somehow different from ours. And she holds the power. All of it. You can't breathe without her knowing about it."

Winnfred sagged. Why did the Primera have to be a power-hungry bitch? "She couldn't have gained control if she came from the past. Something happened. *Nothing* feels right and none of it makes sense."

He nodded. "See what happens when women get the vote? Anarchy and chaos."

***

Mil lay on satin sheets with nothing on but a smile as this month's young stud rose from between her thighs.

"Have I pleased you?"

"Hell, yes, honey. I'm keeping you close for a long time." She winked at him. Yeah, a long time. If history were any indicator, he'd last a month then disappear to Antarctica and instant death. She couldn't risk loose lips ruining her reign. "Much as I would rather linger for another session of your magic, I have too much on my plate today."

Her new lover, nameless like all those before, slid off the bed and stood. She licked her lips. Maybe this one would last two months. The boy was special; he'd actually made her come, multiple times. She sighed as all tight threaded muscle and washboard abs turned, exposing the best buns this side of the Mississippi. Damn, it was fine being the Primera.

She watched him grab his trousers off the floor and headed for her bathroom. Looked like he wouldn't last a week. Everyone knew that room was hers and off limits to even lovers. She rose and strode past him. "Go on now. I'll see you later for a late night celebration," she said, shutting the bathroom door on him.

She leaned against the closed door, her fingers tracing the path of his hands had taken down to the vee between her legs. Too bad he wouldn't last. He was so talented. Still, sex was sex and security was security.

With a shrug, she touched the shower control buttons and stepped under the refreshing, body temperature spray. God, she loved the future. No, not the future, this was her time. She'd simply been born in the wrong century, and she'd corrected that. How her previous model had endured the nineteenth and early twentieth centuries defeated her. Thanks to Doctor Green Sr. for perfecting cloning and transference of all memories and personality. It made ruling so much easier if one never truly aged and could maintain an iron fist on what was left of the country.

Minutes later, Mil slipped on her hand-spun, red silk robe, strode to her dressing table, sat and prepared to give her short reddish blonde hair a good brushing.

Staring at her face, she frowned. In the last six months wrinkles had begun to appear around her eyes. Laugh lines, people called them. But she knew age was once again taking its toll. This time around, the wrinkles were showing up earlier. The original Mil was seventy-seven when she'd been cryoed. The first cloned Mil had lasted until age fifty-six. She patted special moisturizer beneath her eyes and sighed. Looked like this model was only going to make forty.

Bad timing, too. If she weren't careful, she could easily lose all the territory she'd gained in the last forty-four years. With William having been reanimated and cloned ten years ago, then challenging her over what she'd created, she couldn't afford to be re-cloned to twenty-six then euthanized right now. "What the hell. I had to get him out of my life. After all my work, I couldn't let him dismantle my empire."

She thought back to 1941. She'd left explicit orders that she was to be revived when the technology was available to make her young again. She would be the test, William would come later. Much later.

Just forty-four years ago, in 2097 Brock Green's brilliant father finally succeeded in cloning her. Smart man, he never woke the original model, just transferred all her memories. The poor man hadn't seemed very happy with his decision once she'd taken control of the country. Too bad he supposedly got shipped to Antarctica. But she still had his son under her thumb, believing he was actually talking to his father every week.

She cocked her head and tapped her chin with the hairbrush. Lately, Brock had seemed to sour, making snide comments. It was almost as if he knew the truth, yet she was positive he didn't. After all, his father died before sentence was passed and an identical Andro took his place walking onto the plane.

There's no way he's learned the truth. Sometimes, I just don't understand men. Brock had command of all experimental medicine and the largest government-run institute in the country. At least, he'd taken care of her William problem.

She glanced at her wedding photo. "Why couldn't you have just once supported me?"

***

"They could have at least given us books to read, or pen and paper so we could write a journal of our experiences."

"When you're right, Winnie, you're right." Caleb flashed Winnifred a grin. She was a kick-in-the-pants. There she sat on her cot, all starch, her rigid back pressed against the wall, yet he couldn't get the memory of her trim ankles out of his mind.

She thought he hadn't seen her remove her lace-up boots and gartered-silk stockings. She'd been wrong. He'd watched and sweated as she'd slowly rolled each down from above her knees. Now she sat barefoot, her legs curled beneath her on the bed looking ready to play. Caleb's gaze drifted over her face, delightful breasts and down to her bare toes. Sitting in that position, she looked young, naïve, innocent. Not that at twenty-two she was old, but her proud bearing often gave the impression she was older.

"My name is Winnifred."

"Yeah, I know, Winnie. But it makes you sound like a dried-up prune. You aren't an old-maid prig, are you?"

"No," she said in a low growl. "But I hate Winnie. I'm not a—"

"The sound a horse makes. You told me. How about, Win? That makes you a winner."

"Fine, because that's what I am, a winner." She glanced at his hands. Her gaze narrowed on the device he held and she pointed at it. "What's that?"

"Doctor Green said we could read on this." He held up the machine that fit comfortably in his palm. Reaching down with his left hand, he retrieved a second one. "This one's for you." He stood and walked a couple of steps, handed it to her before retreating back to his cot.

She squinted, studying it. "What is it?"

"He called it a 'library card,' and then laughed and said he was trying to explain it in terms we could understand."

Win frowned. "Hmmph. We probably both have higher IQs. What does the machine do?"

Caleb fiddled with it. "He said it contains all the books currently in the Library of Congress."

She gasped. "That has to be millions."

"Add three more zeroes and you'd be closer. There are over a billion."

"That's impossible." Holding her cigarette case holder-sized gizmo, she crossed the room and plopped down next to him. "Show me. … I mean how can it hold all those books when it weighs next to air?"

He chuckled. "Two ounces according to Brock. He said the device projects the image of book pages. You can read from as a regular book. Here's how to turn the pages." He touched the page and swiped his finger across it. "If you want to stop you touch this dot in the right corner and it looks like it folds the page down, acting like a book mark."

"But it won't smell like a book, either." She sniffed. "I love the smell of old books and book stores." She glanced up at him. "I'm not sure this is an improvement." She fiddled with a small dial in its side. "Oh my! Here's a list. Look at all the classics."

"Play with it later. Right now we need to learn about what's happened in the last two hundred years."

She nodded. "May I ask you a question?"

His eyes narrowed. What did she have noodling around in her mind? Heaven help him, it was no telling. "Go ahead."

She glanced up into his eyes. "Why did you really want to marry me?"

He exhaled, closed his eyes and rested his head against the wall. "I wanted to marry you because you're intelligent, you amuse me, keep me on my toes, have a good family name and social position, not to turn you into my *brood mare*. Although I would be less than honest if I didn't admit," his gaze settled on her breasts, "your body excites me." At her humrph, he raised his gaze and flashed her a wicked grin.

"You were rich." She glanced at the skirt of her dress and brushed at it. "You held public office. So why did you really need me?"

Caleb rested his head against the wall and closed his eyes. "I had hoped to run for Congress but … I was raised by a foster father, a simple farmer named Samuel Cash."

"I see." She touched his arm. "But many people are adopted. That is nothing to be ashamed of, nor is being the son of a farmer. He was a righteous man of the soil, or so I suspect. Otherwise you wouldn't be so respectful or have risen in politics as you did."

"I wasn't adopted, I just adopted his name. As righteous or respectful, that isn't a requirement in politics. But Samuel, the dad of my heart, was wonderful. He would have made a great president, but he didn't have those aspirations or political connections. He always said the most important thing in life was the sweet smell of liberty."

"I think I'd like your father a lot."

"Yes, you would have. He died in nineteen-twelve." He raked his hand through his hair. "Understand, I'm proud to call him father and his life mine. It's my life prior to my arrival at the farm that is the problem and could have endangered my future. Marrying you was my insurance policy."

Shifting in her seat so she was facing him, she stared into his eyes. "How so?"

"I'm illegitimate. The result of love tryst between my mother, Julianna and William Davis."

She gasped. "Oh my."

"It gets worse," he said. "Someone, I am assuming my father's wife, wanted my mother and me to disappear. Two men broke into our apartment in the middle of the night. Stabbed my mother to death and dragged me from the room. They were supposed to kill me, too. Instead, they dumped me on an orphan train and sent me on my way as a no-name lone boy to be inspected and claimed by any interested party."

Leaning to one side, Caleb propped himself up with his hand. "I believed I would become no more than an indentured servant except for Samuel and his wife. They truly wanted children. Unfortunately, my adopted mother died of pneumonia that winter. Still, my dad did a wonderful job of raising me." He slapped his hands together. "Story time is now officially over and it's time to close the book on the sad past of one Mr. Caleb Cash."

"Please tell me your father wasn't married to the

Primera."

"Sorry. William Davis is good ole Daddy and Millicent Davis is my bitch of a stepmother."

"She's now—"

"Destroyed liberty and the country the way she did my family."

"What do we do?"

His gaze locked with her moss-green one. "What do we do, indeed?"

Chapter Three

"What do you mean William Davis is cryoed here?" Fran asked.

Brock nodded then winced as her face paled and her hand went to her throat. He hated it when she did that. It meant, she was running scared and rational action might take a back seat. There was no going back now. If they were to survive, Fran had just been elevated to need to know clearance. "I've been taking care of the chamber. Until this minute, no one other than the Primera and I knew he's here."

"How long have you been his doctor?"

"Five years." He took a deep breath. "Of course he wasn't at this facility the entire time."

"Given it's only three years old, that's a fair statement. Where was he before here?"

"In the one I worked at in Illinois. The Primera was

afraid someone would find him."

"Why?"

"The Regime Terrorists were actively trying to take the Capital. And not only was the facility civilian controlled, it was too close to Chicago, her seat of power. So, she built this facility, military controlled and sent me out here—with the body."

"Why are you telling me this now?"

Brock looked over his shoulder and sucked in his breath, letting it out as he realized it was Nicky. "With the exception of the camera covering William, which goes directly to the Primera, every camera monitoring the cryo patients is linked to a reporting network and manned by the SIA."

"I can understand the Primera watching over her husband. But what's the Secret Intelligence Agency have to do with anything?"

"She put all cryos out here, including our unidentified mystery humans, Caleb and Win. I don't know why I didn't see the resemblance immediately. But, trust me, we're dead once someone takes a close look at Caleb. They're going to see William or think Caleb's his clone. They'll kill us just to shut us up." Brock rubbed his forehead. "We have to get out, all of us. They cover the entry and exit points, so we'll need to blind the monitors if we're going to save William."

"Save him?"

"Yeah, save him. You think leaving him here or Caleb or Win here will save us, think again. The Primera iced him when he started lobbying for the return of our civil liberties and constitutional form of government. She can't afford to have him or his son surface."

"Why didn't she just kill him?" Nicky asked as he pulled out a chair and sat between them.

"Nicky's right, why didn't she?" Fran echoed.

"Too many people knew him. Remember, she'd just rammed through the new constitution making William our eternal ruler. She would've lost all power if she took direct action against him. So instead, she had a doctor phony-up a medical for a non-existent disease and put him in stasis until they developed a cure. No way to clone him if the original model's flawed."

"I take it everyone who knows and thinks they'll be cloned is going to meet with the same problem," Nicky said.

"That's my take. Then something will go wrong with the cryo chambers. William will disappear and poof, all her problems disappear including us."

"What's this have to do with us, or should I say Nicky and me?"

Fran's question surprised Brock. He'd never known her to be obtuse. "Because my dear Fran, you've forgotten the succession clause the Primera included in the new constitution." He sighed at hers and Nicky's confused expressions. "The Primera is only the regent. William is the true Primero. With him on ice, any child of his is next in line. And guess who we just reanimated."

"Oh, God, what are we going to do?"

Nicky slapped the table. "I, for one, refuse to have my memory banks wiped."

Brock shot Nicky a glare. Great now their trusted Andro was acting like a histrionic, terrified female. "You're emotional programming hasn't been activated, has it?"

"No. I am still the logical Andro I've always been."

"Right. We'll be safe if we can get out of here. If we want to survive, we have to move fast. All the info on Caleb and Win was sent forward before I knew who they were. Mil's probably assembling her special teams as we speak. And you know what that means. The complex will blow with us inside and it'll be blamed on the *terrorists*."

His shell-shocked companions, now partners in crime, stared blankly at him. Brock stood and began to pace the floor. Nicky rose and trailed behind him imitating Brock's movements.

Brock slapped his hand on the table. "The country is about to change. And for the Primera … I suspect if Caleb and I don't kill her first, William will."

"You want to kill the Primera?"

"Yes, Fran, I want to kill her. Remember my telling you the films of Antarctica were phony?" She and Nicky nodded. "I know because she sent my dad there after he discovered the truth about the breakaway of the west coast and told William. She had an Andro created that could pass for him at a distance, but hadn't done a memory transfer so it didn't know our secret passwords." He stared at the wall over their heads. "My dad never made it to the usual ice death prisoners met in Antarctica. And that's what happens there, the prisoners are pinned outside until they die and then their bodies are burned in ovens."

"If that's what really happens, then your dad had an easier death," Fran whispered.

He pinned them with a glare. "He was tortured and the bitch watched. One of the Constitutionalists was there."

"Constitutionalists?"

"The Primera calls them Regime Terrorists. But their goal is to reinstitute our constitution and civil rights."

"Why was a terrorist there?" Nicky asked.

Brock pinched his nose and closed his eyes, then looked up and met Fran's gaze. "He's part of the government. He was supposed to rescue my dad. He got there too late and couldn't without exposing himself. But he made a copy of the interrogation. If you ever see it you'll understand—" Brock's stomach heaved and he raced for the sink, getting to it just in time.

Fran bolted from the chair and raced to his side. "Let me help you." Wetting a cloth, she placed it on the back of his neck. "We have several problems. If the Primera's monitoring William's chamber, she'll know what we're doing. How can we save William and escape? It takes twenty-four hours to bring a subject out of stasis and with Caleb and Win, it took forty-six."

"They were early subjects." Using the damp towel, he wiped his face. "Nicky, disarm William's cyro monitor from central, it's on a separate line. Then disarm all the rest, including those outside. Put them on a loop. It'll take a while for them to get wise."

"Will do."

"Can you cut in action from the last two days? If so, make it a four to six hour loop. That'll give us some extra time."

"Good idea, Brock. Anything else?"

"I hate to be the harbinger, but what if she's watching us right now? Also how are we going to escape? We've got those blasted implants. If they there's a sixty-one second interruption, the SIA and she will be alerted that we're on to them."

"Actually," Nicky said, "they'll explode."

"They won't explode, I've got that covered. As for The Primera, in Chicago it's the middle of the day. She'll be in her office, analyzing the data and working with General Fizzer on the best way to neutralize us and all her problems. We've got maybe six hours."

He started for the door.

"Wait." Fran stood up. "I told you reviving him will take twenty-four hours."

Brock pivoted and leveled a hard stare. "Nicky, get started on the loops and monitor all military and Primera communications. As for William, he's been cryoed for five years. It shouldn't take more than three hours, Fran."

"Only if we don't follow protocol."

"Screw protocol, Fran. Get with it. It's life or death. William's, Caleb's, Win's and ours. Also, if William dies, we've still got Caleb."

Brock sighed at Fran's shaking hands. The woman was a rock yet extreme apprehension had almost paralyzed her. "We need to get down to the body parts department."

"Why?"

"We're placing our implants in new body part clones and also making sure we have a clone for William so Mil doesn't catch on right away. Let's go." Brock grinned, feeling a sense of freedom for the first time in years.

"Um, Brock, the implants explode if tampered with, remember? Criminals have been trying to get rid of them since the implantations began."

"They don't explode if you get them into another

living human within our sixty second window." Brock winked. "I helped develop the new version. Piece of cake."

"Good. Because," Fran rubbed the back of her neck, "I don't like playing with explosives."

He paused and put his hands on her shoulders. "You are already one. I'm just disarming you."

***

Minutes later, Brock scowled as he rummaged around in the cabinet for a set of surgical instruments. "I don't know why you insisted we do this first."

Fran sat on the side of an exam table in one of the small rooms on the corridor of the building. "Because if I'm going to die, I'd rather do it before we get branded as traitors." Her stomach churned. How she was going to pull this off without bungling something she had no idea. "It's bad enough those guards out there think we're in here for sex."

He shrugged. "It seemed like a good idea. That way we know we won't be interrupted. He stopped and turned around. "Of course we could . . ."

"Don't even go there." She rolled her eyes, but had to admit the thought wasn't totally unattractive. However, it wasn't the place or the time. "You're already going into my neck. I don't really care for you to invade my body anywhere else right now."

He chuckled. "You wouldn't think it was an invasion."

At her stern look, he grabbed the scalpel and approached her. "Can't blame a guy for trying."

"You're a real piece of work," she told him. "For years you've been a sourpuss and now all of a sudden you're a jokester and a regular stand-up comic. Plus, if I'm reading you right, you're sex drive has come back with gusto."

"Maybe so," he murmured as he applied alcohol to the base of her neck. "Just the thought of getting Big Mother far away from me is enough to make me dance. That's my story and I'm sticking to it. Hold onto the table. This might hurt a little bit."

***

"What do you mean William Davis' son is still alive?" Pivoting from the window, Mil drilled Jake Smith, her special agent, with a killing glare. She almost smiled to see him, a former Special Forces Officer, quaking in her presence. Nice to know she hadn't lost her edge.

"The feed from the monitor at Cryo One suggests a man. Caleb Cash, approximately thirty in age, claims to be William Davis's bastard love child."

"Is there more?"

"Yes, ma'am." Her gaze met his until he looked away. "He claims you had his mother killed and shipped him off."

She laughed, allowing the emotion to flow, all of it. Her unwelcome surprise, her frustration, her overwhelming irritation. "Make that lust tryst. The man never could keep it in his pants." She stared into his eyes. "Do away with Caleb whoever-he-is just like we did his mother. Quickly. I want nothing left of the body. Do you understand me. Nothing."

As he turned to leave, she grabbed his arm. "Wait. The others. Have you checked the microchips? Is everyone present and accounted for?"

He nodded. "Yes, Madam Primera. All personnel on duty as assigned."

She eased her grip. "Fine. Then no one has jumped to conclusions. We'll have to dispel their doubts should they begin to surface." She walked out the door of the observation center and stopped before her senior agent. "Frank, in the bubble. We need to talk."

He nodded, walking to the side but asking no questions, remaining silent. A good trait in a man. Within minutes they entered her special conference room, the windowless, lead-lined one with a raised glass and carbon-fiber scrambler throughout the entire structure. "Don't forget to leave you shoes, jacket and everything in your pockets over there." She pointed to a bench against the wall. "Then go through the body scanner."

"You've added new security."

"For a reason. We found Regime terrorists had planted bugs." She watched the monitor as Frank passed through the scanner. He was clean. Once he was seated, she sat at the head of the table. "I've given Jake a delicate mission. It concerns information that can never get out. Once he's completed the job, I'll contact you."

She leaned forward, knowing how she looked. She should. She'd practiced the hard-core bitch who could kill her own mother without a second thought by practicing in front of the mirror. "Make him disappear ... permanently. No body, no bones, nothing, not a cell of DNA is to remain."

His drooping, hound dog eyes grew to the size of huge saucers. "Pardon me, Madam Primera, but Jake has been with you since you came into office and he has always been—"

"Did you hear what I ordered?"

He bowed his head. "Yes, ma'am. I'll take care of it immediately, Madam Primera."

"Good." She smiled. "It's reassuring to know I can count you, Frank. I'd hate for anything to happen to you."

Minutes later, Mil eased into her bedroom and quietly shut the door behind her. Focused on only one thing, she charged across to her walk-in closet and pushed the button to the automatic folding doors.

She'd set-up William's monitor in the one place no one went but her. By being here in the closet, she knew none of her boy-toys would ever be that much the wiser.

Mil walked through the fifteen by fifteen foot space to the back end where a console table stood. William's monitor was front-and-center. But the others for the cryo unit and its sister facility in Kentucky were also there. No one knew she had a duplicate set watching as the SIA did. It was to ensure accuracy in their reporting.

First, she set the monitor for the observation unit back by a few hours. A man and woman sat there in clothing from the time period of her previous existence. Her gag reflex activated. How she'd hated that restrictive clothing. She noted the woman was a very attractive redhead, slightly darker hair than her own, and of regal bearing. Then she focused in on the man. Terror striking her core, she realized it was indeed Caleb Cash. Damn the man, he had more lives than an alley cat.

She slammed her fist down on the table. "Why couldn't you have died on some dirt farm?" All these years he'd survived. He'd even been cryoed. They'd said they had a test couple in 1941. That scientist and her assistant had insisted it was the best for science, for future technology. But had never mentioned who they were. But if he was not one of that twosome, then how in the hell had Caleb stayed so young? How was he even alive? No one got cloned without her permission.

Mil pulled down the files dealing with the original cryo experiments. As she leafed through literature on the events from the time of her first cryo, she'd spotted the information about Caleb and the woman. They'd been found in a cave in a suspended animation state. As they started to rouse, it was decided to use them as the first cryo patients. They were the guinea pigs. Since they didn't die, the scientists went on to put her and William under.

For years, fear had consumed her that Caleb would show up on their doorstep one day and tell William the truth. She'd learned after Julianna's death not to leave loose ends. The killers and Caleb. She'd gotten lucky with the killers. Times were different then. If you were hired to do a job and were paid in full, it was a done deal. But Caleb, he'd been a wild card. If he'd shown up at the door, William would have kicked her to the curb. At Caleb's disappearance in 1918, surprise and delight filled her.

He disappeared only to return now like a wraith.

Mil continued to stare at the live Caleb in the observation area. He looked exactly like William had at that age, both times. Although angry beyond bounds, she had to admit she was intrigued by the man and his intelligence. He'd hidden his hand well in a game of cat-and-mouse, hiding his fortune before he disappeared. The money apparently had been hidden by Caleb himself. He'd then left a will behind saying no trace would be found of the money unless he was proven to be dead beyond a shadow of a doubt by producing a body. To this day his assets remained frozen in a location yet unknown. If it were currency, he was out of luck. She chuckled. "Go to sleep rich, wake up in the gutter."

Caleb was smart. Too smart. She supposed as he grew in power and prestige he'd known she would discover he was still alive and conspire to have him removed permanently. It was his last parting shot at her. His grand hurrah.

Turning it back to current time, she looked at the image and froze. Her eyes narrowed on the two techs who walked down the hall. She'd swear she'd seen them an hour ago.

She punched a button. "Check cryo unit one-ten-fory-two. Make sure the security camera is focused on that unit. Ten minutes later she stared at her husband's face through the frosted window over his face and smiled.

Once Frank and his team took care of Caleb, all her problems would be over.

Chapter Four

Win glanced at to Caleb. "What's with Nicky? The past hour he's been laughing and crying out 'Free at last. Free at last. Thank God, almighty we're free at last?'"

"Haven't a clue given he's free and we aren't." Frowning, he snorted. "Hell, we can't even go to the can alone."

"Did he say anything last time he escorted you to the washroom?"

"Yes. You won't believe it. He said, 'Be ready, we're blowing this joint.'"

"Blowing a joint? What does that mean?"

"He said it was slang for getting out of here quickly without anyone knowing it."

"Really? Do you know when?"

He rose from his cot and walked to the opening then paced back to her. "No. Nicky wouldn't do anything without Green or Victor's permission. So, I take it we're waiting on them, and from what the guards were muttering as they passed us, it'll be awhile." He raised a hand halting her next question. "Seems they're busy in the parts room 'pleasuring each other'."

"I don't believe it. Not if we're escaping."

"Get over it, Win." He smiled.

"But sex?"

He sighed. "Yes, tragic. Wish I'd thought of it. It's a great stress reliever."

She stood, her fists on her hips. "If you are alluding to us, must I remind you we aren't married?"

"If I remember correctly, you said you wouldn't marry me until hell froze over. Which, of course, it did." Grinning, he licked his lips. "Sex doesn't absolutely require marriage as my parents figured out."

"Well," she said, "It does for me, so get those lascivious thoughts out of your mind."

"I'll try. No guarantees," he murmured as Brock and Fran walked up and the force field disappeared with a shushing sound.

"How is our escape coming along?" Win asked.

Fran stared at Brock, a frown on her face. "If Nicky has said anything—"

"No, not a word," Caleb said. "Ignore her. Sometimes the woman talks out of her mind. Where are we going and how many of us?"

Glancing at the ceiling, Brock scowled. "The four of us plus Nicky. Don't say anything or hint to anyone else we're leaving."

"We're going on the lam."

"Why don't you just blurt it out without checking if we're alone?" Brock exhaled then turned back to them. "Fran and Nicky are taking you out the back door. You'll make a short stop at her apartment for her to gather some things where I'll join you shortly."

"What then?" Caleb asked. He wanted to trust these three but he didn't like the secrecy. "And why are we doing this?"

He nodded. "Your lives are in danger. The Primera didn't know we were going to reanimate you, wake you. Fran didn't get approval. Now, our lives along with yours are in the crapper."

"But what are we going to do?" Win asked. "We have no proper housing and no money at all."

Caleb smiled. "I can provide the money."

Brock shook his head. "You may have hidden some currency, but the currency you have no longer has value except to a collector."

"Don't worry about it."

***

"Where's Doctor Green? Isn't he coming with us?" Caleb asked as they climbed into a funny looking contraption with wings. Much as he wanted to trust these doctors and Nicky, he didn't. He'd long ago learned no one helped another without expectation or gain.

"Brock is reanimating someone the Primera hates. Her enemies have a habit of disappearing and if Brock doesn't save him, he's dead. Don't worry, they'll join us later. The key right now is to save you. Fasten your harnesses please," she said, staring in the rearview mirror.

"Harnesses?" Win looked around the carriage. "I don't see any."

Fran chuckled. "Just push the small button on the armrest to your left.

As Caleb pushed both Win's and his buttons, amazement filled him as two straps joined in the middle dropped from the ceiling of the vehicle and snapped in place securing them to the seat. "Clever. Is this your version of the Model T?"

Fran shook her head. "Heavens no. That was a car. This is a water jet car." She laughed. "Some comics call them 'Wet-jets' after a gizmo they had … never mind. Anyway, it flies. Its fuel is water, actually steam. No waste or pollution."

She pushed another button and the machine lifted off the ground and whizzed along the breezeway. Caleb chuckled at Win's sudden intake of breath. "Oh my. This is fun. You must teach me how to operate it."

"If we're to survive, we have to learn more about this world and who has power and how we can unseat Mil, first," Caleb ordered. "Fun can come later. People have microchips implanted in them so the police can track them, Fran, aren't they going to find you and the doctor."

"Not anymore." Fran smiled.

Nicky beamed. "Me neither."

"We've removed the microchips. That's what we were doing just before we left."

"I thought you two were having—"

"A planning session. I see the guards bought our excuse and were quick to spread the news," Fran snickered.

"I know this is a stupid question," Caleb said. "Does the jet have microchips, too? And did you disable them?"

The jet slowed as Fran beat her head against the steering wheel and repeatedly muttered, "Oh, shit. Oh, shit. Oh, shit." She lifted her head and looked at them, blinking back tears. "We have to ditch this sucker before they realize we're in it."

"I can blow the circuits," Nicky said.

"Do it now. We'll ditch it a mile from my place. But we can't risk using it again. There'll be a record of it that the SIA can use to find us."

"How about horses?" Caleb asked. "They don't put microchips in them, too, do they?"

***

"Where are we going?" William asked.

Brock approached Mach 2 as he turned the machine on a sharp curve. "To a colleague's home. She's picking up a few things for the trip. Before we arrive, you need to know a few things."

"No doubt, especially what Mil's been up to over the past five years." William frowned. "I'd just been learning about the previous thirty-one years when she iced me." He leaned against the seat and closed his eyes. "Get on with it."

"Your son, Caleb's alive."

William's eyes flew open. "What? Mil told me he died with Julianna in …" His voice trailed off.

"Exactly." Brock glanced over at him. "Mil told you he was dead. You never checked. You just took her word for it. Didn't you?"

"I wonder if she's ever told me the truth about anything. I wonder if she ever loved me."

"I doubt it." He saw the man's eyes redden. "The fact Caleb's alive is really quite remarkable." He quickly told him the story behind Caleb and Win's survival.

"I see. Did she know about Caleb being found? Is that why the two were cryoed top secret?"

He shrugged. "I don't know. With your investments and money, you two more or less ran the government even back then. Money can do wonders. Mil probably used them as guinea pigs to see if the cryo actually placed you in stasis or killed you."

"You said there was another person found in the cave with Caleb. Who is she?"

"Winnifred Marshall's a very attractive green-eyed redhead. I'm not sure why she was with Caleb, but I can only assume they were linked romantically in some capacity."

"Winnifred Marshall?" he asked. "Are you sure?"

Brock nodded. "That's what she said her name was."

He smiled. "How appropriate. If you read your history, Brock, you'll discover that a large group of Suffragettes formed the Marshall Movement in late 1918 after one of their sisters in the cause mysteriously disappeared. The movement is credited with being the true force behind women getting the right to vote."

***

"I like your place, Fran. Clean, not cluttered. I've always loved minimalism and always hated those doilies and trinkets of my time," Caleb said, then grinned when Win shot him a scowl. The woman could be riled so easily.

"Yes, it's very nice, but is there a law against displaying photographs of family in this time?" Win asked.

"No." Fran threw some clothes in a backpack. "But ten years ago when I lost my entire family in the earthquake, I couldn't handle looking at their faces every day. I keep small ones of my mom and dad and brother in the locket around my neck."

"What earthquake?" Win sat on the corner of Fran's bed and scooted up to the headboard.

Fran paused. "Sorry, I guess we've been bombarding you with nothing but information since you woke up. Ten years ago, September 2131, there were hundreds, maybe thousands, of simultaneous underground nuclear explosions along the San Andreas Fault and adjacent faults throughout the west. They also took out everything from a part of Mexico all the way up to the western most part of Alaska, creating a new west coast."

"I'm so sorry about your family."

"Thanks." Fran stared blankly at the pile of clothes.

"What happened? You say, it took out part of a quarter of the country. How?"

Fran glanced at Caleb. "I always thought it was the regime terrorists, those who hated Mil Davis, who were responsible."

"Regime terrorists?" Win asked.

"I understand their hatred," Caleb sneered. "But you haven't told us what happened."

"After what Brock told me a few hours ago, I now understand, too. But not back then. I was like everyone else. The country hadn't recovered from the Yellowstone

Cauldron eruption when Mil came on the scene in 2097. She helped us rebuild and get going. She accomplished in thirty-one years what no one else could during the preceding hundred."

"Why would they hate her for saving the country?"

Caleb glanced over his shoulder at them. "Maybe because she's an insane murderer,"

"You're right, and not because of her hiring men to kill your mother. But because she was behind the explosions that destroyed our country and most of the world. Also, it seems the terrorists are really freedom fighters called Constitutionalists."

Arms wrapped around her knees, Win rocked back and forth on the bed. "What happened to our country afterwards?"

Fran grabbed a few more clothes and threw them in the carry-all. "Mil used the loss of a hundred fifty million citizens and the entire west coast to establish a totalitarian state during the chaos. All Americans reached for hope and a strong figure to bring their world back into balance."

Caleb turned from the window and stared at them. "It doesn't surprise me. The woman's already proven she'll kill to get what she wants."

"One person, Caleb." Win stared at him. "Your mother. And she didn't kill you. How can you believe she caused it?"

Eyes closed, Caleb rested his head against the wall. For a woman involved in Women's Suffrage, Win not only had a soft heart but was naïve. "She ordered my death. Her thugs figured she'd never know they'd gotten paid twice. They figured dumping me on the orphan train fulfilled her order to get rid of me."

Win clutched her throat. "How could anyone purposely destroy land on that enormous of a scope and annihilate so many innocent Americans in the name of power?"

Fran shrugged. "She wouldn't be the first. Hitler, Stalin, Pol Pot of the Khmer Rouge, they all did it."

"Who are they?"

Fran sighed. "Sorry, after your time. Look at the Armenian Holocaust. Not on the same scale as those three, but bad enough."

Win rested her chin on her knees. "Why can't people remember history and refuse to repeat the same mistakes?"

"It's a genetic flaw, I guess." Fran paused. "Good research topic. If we live through this, maybe I'll study it."

Caleb glanced at them. "I remember how the San Francisco earthquake was followed by the firestorms that almost destroyed the city. Is that what happened this time?"

"No. The explosions triggered massive quakes that ruptured the earth to such a degree everything slid into the

Pacific. Those not in the immediate quake zone drowned in the tidal wave that crashed over the open desert and formed a new coastline."

Win stared up at her, her eyes shielded by wet lashes. "At least, they didn't suffer."

She nodded. "That's what I've always told myself."

Caleb crossed the room to the bed and sat beside Win. Without thought, he took her hand and his thumb caressed her knuckles. "How did you manage to survive, Fran?"

"I was at the University of Chicago attending Medical School. Thankfully I wasn't on east coast. New York City, Washington, DC and most heavily populated areas down our eastern coastline were wiped out by the tidal waves that followed for three days. Over the last past years, people started drifting back, trying to re-establish." Fran turned and strode into the bathroom.

Win grabbed his hand. "What's happened to our world?"

"It's disappeared. I suspect all the smaller island nations are gone along with a lot of Europe and Asia. Makes for easier world conquest."

"Mil's insane."

"Yeah, I know. Only now instead of focusing on my mom and me, she's taking on the world."

Hearing Fran return, Caleb glanced at her and spotted

her red eyes. She was in pain, and as much as he'd like to ignore the dead horse in the middle the room, let her lick her wounds and not ask another question, he couldn't. If he and Win were going to survive Mil and this new world, they needed information, a lot of it and fast. "Where's the capital, now?"

"Chicago."

"When can we go there?" Win asked.

"If you want to live, stay away from it. The moment Mil Davis gained control the whole city went under military shutdown. No one gets in or out of Chicago. She claims it's for the protection of the government. The truth is she's turned the city into one big experiment."

Win gasped. "Like what? I mean, the cryo institute is way out here in Nevada."

"Her experiments aren't for the benefit of mankind," Fran threw a shirt in the pack. "Her experiments are designed for military readiness. I've heard she's set her sights on Canada and then Mexico. Once she controls everything from the Arctic to the tip of Argentina, she can branch out overseas."

"Don't forget what's left of Alaska," Caleb said. "No doubt it's still a big land mass."

Fran smiled. "It was our forty-ninth state. Of course we lost our fiftieth, Hawaii, in the quake's aftermath. Tidal waves go both ways."

"Alaska makes sense. It has plenty of gold and other resources." Caleb leveled Fran a stare.

Win pulled free and stood. "I wonder if Nicky has finished getting all our food goods together."

"I would think so." Fran zipped her case closed. She fit a blond wig over her dark brown hair, then threw some clothes at Win. "Put these on and here's some dye for your hair. You don't want to draw attention to yourself. That red hair is already a beacon."

"She's not dying her hair." Caleb slid his fingers through Win's hair, lifted it up and let it drift down around her shoulders. "I love it. It's like a summer fire. Do something else."

"I'll put it up and under a hat if you have one."

Fran handed her another wig. "Use this instead."

She laughed. "I'll be another woman. I've always loved the name Grace." Win glanced at him. "There are no short and ugly nicknames." At his grin, she turned back to the jean jeans Fran had tossed her. "I can't get over that women have the freedom to wear pants. I believe I'll like this part."

"So will I." Caleb winked. "Finally no more wondering what's hidden under those long skirts."

She fiddled with braiding her hair. "By the way, what makes that man Brock's saving so important? There have to be a lot of important people at the facility."

112

Fran nodded. "Some. It was used to store only a few high value individuals. You two plus this man. He has the power to bring down the Primera."

Caleb straightened. "If he has that kind of power, he has my support."

***

Caleb stood in the kitchen as he and Nicky went through what the Andro had bought. "Does everyone eat these Reserve Rations now?"

"Brock said to buy them, so I bought them."

"I hope they taste better than they did in 1918."

Nicky laughed as he packed the meals in a silver-lined bag. "These are very different from those. If my memory banks are accurate, and they always are, these 2572s are so named because they can be stored until that year. They're activated by direct sunlight and a drop of water. Immediate expansion and they're reconstituted and are ready to consume. That's why we have to keep them in this bag."

William scratched his chin. "What's inside the bag, silver?"

Nicky shook his head. "It's a new carbon alloy. It's almost weightless and light deflecting properties."

"Does it harm the planet?" Caleb hated the way people in his time ruined the planet, covered Mother Earth with buildings, ruined its water, ruined the air. Having lived on a farm, his first thought was always conservation.

From what Fran had told them, with Mil as the Primera destroy the world to rule it was the imperative.

"Oh, heavens no," Nicky said. "That wouldn't be very brown and this world is all about brown."

He frowned. "What's brown?"

Nicky closed the bag. "Of the earth. All products must be made from the earth so they can return to the earth." He hefted the bag on his shoulder. "We're done. Let's go back to the main room. Brock's water-jet landed on the front landing stip."

"How in God's name did you hear that?"

Nicky grinned. "Supersonic hearing. It's a gift."

Chapter Five

"What am I going to say to my son?" William clenched his hands as they approached the front door. Nausea assailed him. He ground his back teeth. Vomiting on Caleb's feet was not the first image of him he wanted his son to have of their reunion.

"I don't know. You sure can't say, 'Daddy's home.' I think it would be best if you just tell him the truth."

"What if he doesn't believe me?"

"You've got to be kidding me." Brock glanced over at him. "If he can buy he was in stasis for more than thirty years, then cryogenically frozen by the government and successfully revived in 2141, he should believe you didn't know what happened."

William's lips twitched. "You have a point.

"Just be prepared to make the argument of your life in case he holds a grudge."

As Nicky opened the door, William saw two women and his son gathered around their gear.

Brock nodded to William. "You go first. You can do this."

Clearing his throat and squaring his shoulders, he stepped in front of Brock. As his gaze met Caleb's, he knew his son. They were now almost the same age, yet there was no denying who he was. Except for his lips which were Julianna's, they could pass for twins.

"You!" Caleb said, his lips flattened and eyes lost all their warmth, turning hard and flinty. He clenched and unclenched his fists.

"Caleb," William said, "it's critical you listen to me before thinking you know what happened."

"Really? Let's see if we're both talking about the same thing. Your wife hired some thugs who murdered my mother."

"Mil told me you and your mother died of consumption, Caleb."

Caleb laughed, but the laugh was anything but filled with mirth. It rattled from his throat like a death march. "It's amazing how one can confuse consumption with the sharp end of a blade gutting a person," he snarled.

William's blood drained from his face, acid crawled up his throat. Tears burned his eyes at the image of his beautiful Julianna's death and Caleb's desolation. "I swear,

Caleb, I didn't know. I didn't know." He collapsed onto a chair, sobbing, and then winced as Winnifred Marshall knelt beside him and placed her hand on his shoulder.

"It is a sad day, sir, when your kin sees fit to murder a loved one." Win glanced over her shoulder. "Caleb, can't you see your father wasn't an accomplice in your mother's demise or your abduction."

His heart hammering like a farrier, William sought his son's gaze. "Abduction? Where did they take you, son?" Hope sprang in William when Caleb's face softened as they stared at each other.

"To the orphan train. I was shipped to Illinois."

"Were the people who took you in kind?"

Caleb nodded. "I am proud I was raised by them."

William smiled, the pain of this whole sordid tale still piercing his heart. He stood and held out his hand. "I know you haven't forgiven me, but for now will you simply acknowledge that I had no evil intent?"

"Yes." He grasped William's hand. "It'll take longer to forgive your negligence in not confirming your wife's story. Given who she is, you should have known better."

He nodded. "You're right. I did confirm Millicent's story with my man, Robert. It seems she'd bought his loyalty. However, I thank you for what you're willing to give."

Win stood and hugged William. "I forgive you for it

117

all," she said softly. "I can tell your heart is pure. It's said I have the sight."

He smiled. "She's a fine woman, Caleb," he said. "You should marry her."

At Caleb's smirk and her blush, William knew this was a bone of contention.

"I understand Mil's acting as regent in your name but how do you have the power to bring her down?" Caleb asked.

"Because she foolishly made me the ruler, in other words, the king, and any off-spring I had as my heir." William's eyes narrowed and forehead furrowed. "You are not only my son, but the spitting image of me. She can't allow you to live … or me. And, if I know my wife, and I unfortunately do, she's onto us already. So I suggest we contact my allies. Fast."

***

"Damn, it's hot. And it's nine at night."

"It's the desert, son."

Caleb shot William a shut-the-hell-up glare and turned back to Green. "How much further and are you sure it's secure?" He wasn't worried about himself; he'd learned to take care of himself on the orphan train. But if anything happened to Win, Green didn't need to worry about the Primera because Caleb would skin the man alive.

"It's a place just outside of Hawthorne, less than a

mile from here. It's also great. We can hide and plan," Brock said.

"Okay, that tells me where but not why you think it's secure or why Mil, William's *beloved* wife won't find us."

"It used to be an old bunker to store missiles during the Cold War. But don't worry, this bunker's missile free."

Caleb strode alongside Win, his hand on her elbow, through the desert sand. "*This* bunker?"

"The one we're going to is in the middle of a number of them which still have active missiles. When my dad showed me this area, he said Mil's unaware any of the silos are empty." Brock chuckled. "She'll never think to look for us here."

"I sure didn't know about it." William placed his hand on Win's other elbow in an attempt to keep her upright. "Unless she's discovered them in the last five years, you're right, we'll be safe."

Nicky lifted Fran up in his arms. "There's nothing in my memory banks about this location or the missiles."

Win glanced over her shoulder at them. "If Nicky Andro doesn't know about it, it has my vote."

Fran lifted her head off Nicky's chest. "We're walking across flat land with no cover, not even scrub and are open targets if the Primera institutes marshal law and a curfew. If we want to survive, we'd better approach every step with caution and watch out for POPs."

"Who the heck is Pops?" Win asked.

Caleb was worried about Fran. She didn't look good. A glassy gaze and pinched expression didn't bode well. She'd tripped an hour ago and had twisted her ankle. Thank God the doc had his medical equipment with him and had wrapped her ankle.

Fran dropped her head, resting it against Nicky's chest. "Police for Peace, they're the national police force. Most of them used to patrol the Mexican border for illegal immigrants. These days no Mexican in his right mind wants to be within a hundred miles of our country."

Caleb's jaw clenched. Damn, that's all they needed. It was bad enough Mil and her goons were on them. But the POPs carried an air of authority that secret police never did, unless ... "Do they wear uniforms?"

"No." William exhaled sharply. "Sorry, that was my idea. I thought having them undetectable made sense. It still does, but it's not to our advantage." He looked around at the group. "Since Brock knows the bunker's exact location, I suggest we split into two groups. Brock can give its coordinates to Nicky and he can carry Fran, because she can't walk. Brock, you take the other. Smaller groups won't draw that much attention."

"Great idea. If we're considered terrorists then let's maneuver like insurgents," Caleb said. "How do you want to split up?"

"I'll take Win with me," Fran said.

Knots formed in Caleb's stomach and his palms grew clammy at the thought of Win alone, without him. "I'll stay with Fran. I look enough like William if stopped they might let us pass. Women on their own draw trouble, especially Win. I suspect these POPs are a law unto themselves, functioning like vigilantes."

Win's chin jutted out and glared at him. "I am no more trouble than you and William. Remember, that power-hungry woman wants us all dead."

"We'll only be separated for an hour, at most." William said. "Win appears to be bright and capable to me. Leave her with Fran and let Nicky help them. The two of us can go with Brock."

Caleb's lips thinned and eyes narrowed. He was trapped. Only Nicky could carry Fran through this desert. He didn't need water and didn't tire. "I see the logic of Fran staying with Nicky. But my suggestion is William goes with them. And Win and I stay with Brock. Two men, one woman. We're short water."

"I can carry my own weight," Win snapped.

"I'm not arguing about this Win. You aren't sweating like you were. Dehydration's setting in."

"I agree." Brock gave Nicky exact GPS coordinates.

Win reached out and squeezed Caleb's hand. "I know you only wish to protect me, but, believe me, I have been a fighter since I took my first breath. I will be safe."

His gaze locked on her moss green eyes, shining in the moonlight. He smiled faintly. "I'll never let anything happen to you, Win." He pressed a soft kiss on her lips. "Your beauty isn't skin deep. It glows from the inside out." He brushed strands of the wig's long, curly brown - hair from her face.

Her knees buckled at his words. "You are becoming a charmer Caleb Cash."

"I certainly hope so. You're mine, Win. You always have been and a couple hundred years hasn't changed that."

"Then let me go with Fran and Nicky. It's night, Caleb. I'll be fine for an hour or two."

"Come now, children," William said. "Time's passing."

Caleb turned to his father. "I am almost your age, you know."

William shook his head. "Perhaps in body years, but my mind's filled with almost ninety years. Although it feels like centuries."

"All humans experience this," Nicky said. "Back in 2076, we discovered that the mind is actually a consciousness separate from the body that stays intact even after the bodily functions, brain activity and respirations have ceased. It is as if the soul, for lack of a better term, never dies but floats in another dimension only waiting for its emergence into a new life."

Fran punched his shoulder. "Too much information for right now, Nicky."

Nicky made a motion across his lips then said, "I know where we're going, so Win, Fran and I will travel north, then east."

Brock nodded. "We'll go south, then east and cut back north to the bunker."

"Here's to our freedom." Caleb handed Win his water. "I love you."

***

Mil stared at the monitor in her closet and knocked it from the shelf. The screen broke, shards of glass spilling across the carpet. "Shit! A loop! It has to have been going for a few hours." She braced herself against a rack of clothes, her hands fisted, ready to punch out the first person she saw. William was alive and awake. "Damn, damn, damn, damn." She stomped around the closet, avoiding the glass.

Now what? He'd been briefed. No doubt about it. He was now aware of her duplicity and betrayal. She knew him well. He'd be out for blood, probably already in route to Chicago. But now his bastard son had joined him in vengeance. They'd be on a mission, for it was personal.

How did she play it? What was her next move? She took a deep breath. *They're not as smart as me and they're not in power*. Nor would they be if she played her cards right. She bit her lower lip. For all anyone knew, they were mere Andros impersonating the real people. No, they didn't stand a chance as long as she stayed one step ahead of them. Did they?

"Where are you going, William?" she asked out loud. It was time for a special SIA intervention, her best man. Time to summon Special Agent Hood.

Chapter Six

An explosion shook the ground. "What the hell," Caleb shouted as they all turned as one and looked behind them. Billowing flames and a huge plume of smoke rose in the distance.

"That was the institute," Brock said. "They initiated the self-destruct."

"She knows we're not there."

Brock clapped William on the shoulder. "But she thinks you are. The clone, remember."

"Damned bitch!" he ground out through gritted teeth. "That was meant to erase me as a problem from her life."

Caleb snorted. "Welcome to my world, *Dad*. Still think she has any feeling for you?"

"This is war," William said. "That bitch is going down."

"We need strategy. Once we're safe in the bunker, we plot out how to get hold of some of my gold."

"Is it all in one place?" Brock asked.

Caleb rolled his eyes. "Give me some credit. Only a fool puts all their assets in one location."

"We can't take it all with us if the assets are all gold bars, but one should do the trick."

"Where's the closest location?"

Caleb met his dad's gaze and shrugged. "The closest one is Santa Fe. Although I think the location in San Antonio is a safer choice at the moment."

"How do you know these deposits of monumental treasure haven't been removed or tampered with and covered up?" Brock snorted. "It's been more than two-hundred years since you hid your fortune."

Caleb struggled to keep a snarl from his voice. He was getting tired of these doctors and William thinking he didn't have two brain cells to rub together. "Trust me. They haven't been disturbed."

"I have complete faith in you, son."

"You're right about San Antonio," Brock said as he trudged forward. "Even in post-apocalyptic America, Texas is still a wild, untamed country."

William chuckled. "Mil used to scream how herding rats was easier than reining in all those cowboys."

"I'm assuming horses won't seem odd in either

location," Caleb said.

"Right." Brock checked his handheld tracking device, the one he called GPS. "We're fifteen minutes from the bunker. We should get there before the eyes in the sky pick us up." He made a sharp turn east. "In five minutes we turn north and will arrive at the bunker within another ten minutes."

"Good. I'm not sure how much more time we have. What form's the gold in, son?"

"A thousand ingots weighing twenty pounds each and fifty thousand twenty-four carat twenty dollar Liberty Double Eagle gold coins."

"Liberty Double Eagles?" squeaked Brock.

"Yes, why?"

"Because, son, they're rarer and worth more than an ingot. And they're easier to transport."

"And easier to use when bribing."

William roared. "You are my son."

"Some mineral assay locations are still operating in Texas. We can turn one coin into over a million dollars' worth of tokens and hologram cards."

"Tokens and hologram cards?" Caleb asked.

William nodded. "Tokens complete with the bitch's face on them. Our new ludicrous currency is made of tin. The hologram card is a non-duplicative card with whatever value you can support loaded into it. You can use it at any

127

place of business by waving it next to an item you wish to purchase."

Caleb sighed. "Looks like the economy is a mess."

"You have no idea," Brock said.

"No offense, Brock, but we'll use my contacts to change the Eagle into tokens and renewable cards."

Caleb jerked free of William's hand on his shoulder. "That kind money is going to attract Mil's and her hangmen, sorry, your security's attention."

"The funds will be kept in Lichtenstein and renewed as needed. As of five years ago, Mil hadn't broken their banking system."

"How can you be so sure."

"Because I set up accounts there to fund the Constitutionalists and they're still solvent. Otherwise, they wouldn't still exist."

***

"Are you saying Mil Davis blew the institute and knows we aren't there?" Win grabbed Nicky's arm. "I mean, you said she wouldn't know. You had everything on a loop."

"Yes. And it was only a matter of time before security realized what they were seeing was a loop. I just bought us time."

"But she thinks William was." Fran said. "The Primera must have wanted to ice her husband something fierce.

But, if she really did it, she has a backup plan to ensure she remains in power. Let's slip into the bar over there and see if they have their interphase on. With the blast, people will tune into the news. Put me down, Nicky, otherwise we'll draw too much attention."

"But—"

"Put my boot on and just hold onto my elbow."

"I could use some water and Caleb's canteen is almost empty." Win sighed. "I'm drier than a skeleton in the middle of the desert."

Fran laughed. "Hate to break it to you, but we're in the desert." She stopped and stared back at Win. "And for God's sake, keep the canteen hidden in your pack, that'll really draw too much attention. Also, don't say anything if you can help it, unless someone just says hi. In fact, why don't you let me say you're mute. Yeah, you're mute, that be safer."

"Just for the record, I would never divulge any information."

Fran smiled. "Good, but if you don't speak it makes it easier for me to order Nicky to stay silent also."

"See what I have to put up with?" Nicky muttered. "I really am very abused."

Win smiled as they entered the bar. It was all wood and old fixtures. It fit in with the ones of her era. At amy rate, they were like the photos she'd seen of them, because no Suffragette entered this kind of establishment. No need to give their enemies ammunition to use against them. Plus some of those women wanted to abolish all alcohol. While she might not have agreed with Caleb about most things, she did in his claim that imposing one's belief of abstinence on the country was just plain wrong.

Her eyes narrowed on the ten foot screen that covered most of one wall. Now that was something they didn't have in 1918. With a gasp, she saw the image of Mil Davis on the screen talking. "Is that a motion picture?"

"No. It isn't film. It's happening in real time, right now, but she's not here. I'll explain later. No talking. You're mute, remember?" Fran whispered as they stood just inside the doorway, staring at the broadcast.

"I have interrupted this local news broadcast, to report that our cryo institute, Time After Time, in Hawthorne, Nevada has been viciously destroyed by a band of Regime Terrorists. Citizens in the area should not be alarmed. The Police for Peace have already captured six of the terrorists and will ensure they are imprisoned. As for the ringleaders, they are still on the loose." Mil paused and dabbed at her eyes.

Her face faded as a picture of William Davis showed on the screen. "Before blowing up the institute they woke my husband and have taken him captive," Mil's voice caught on a sob, her hand holding the linen cloth once again dabbed her eyes.

"This doesn't look good," whispered Win.

"No, shit, Sherlock," hissed Fran. "And shut up, you're mute."

"As you know fellow citizens, he had been cryoed to protect him until a cure could be found for his disease. Now, I fear he is dying and held captive along with two recently cryoed patients."

Video from the observation room popped up before Win's eyes and she sucked in her breath. "The ringleaders of this terrorist cell appear to be none other than the doctors at the institute Doctors Brock Green and Fran Victor." Their faces popped up on the monitor.

Fran ducked her head.

"With that short blond wig, you're a different person."

"Shush. You're mute, remember?" Fran hissed.

Mil's face reappeared on the screen. "If you see any of these people, please notify the POPs at once or signal us at the locator showing at the bottom of the screen. Remember my husband and the young couple are innocent hostages. They are not to be harmed. If possible, I would prefer the terrorists be handled in an appropriate and humane manner, by being imprisoned in Antarctica."

Fran grabbed Win. "Sorry about the water, you'll have to wait until we get to our rendezvous. Let's get out of here before someone recognizes us."

"Remember, that screen is two way. We have time, my interface says it isn't two way right now. But if security spots us, you're dead and I'm wiped," Nicky muttered.

"I have created a reward of a million dollars for the safe return of William and the young couple. The government has issued a million dollar bounty, dead or alive, on the doctors."

Nicky rested his arms around Fran and Win as they exited and slowed their escape to a casual saunter down the sidewalk.. "Walk, don't run."

***

The bunker door screeched as it lifted on an automatic system. "Sure doesn't sound like it's been opened for a while"

"Right in one." Brock pushed inside. "I doubt it's been used since around 2078 when those cowboy oil men pushed for war against Iran."

Caleb froze. "You fought another country for black gold?" In his time countries went to war over land, not oil.

"No. Prior to any action, the water jet was invented and solar collectors were placed in space. Within a few years, no one used oil and then the wars really began. Back then things were different. Come on. Shut the door behind you, William. It's the red button."

Caleb shone the laser plutonic light inside the clean cavity. As the hatch creaked shut, running lights clicked on along the floor.

Within minutes, bright white lights lit inside the building. Caleb froze. The interior was huge, larger than his cave, with shiny metal walls reflecting the light like a mirror.

"Nothing can get in this baby." Brock slapped a wall. "The silo has a self-contained air supply with scrubbers." He opened doors lining the side of one wall.

"Ah, see?" Caleb pointed to a large, green-lettered sign that read *oxygen valve*. "Given there are only five of us, this should supply sufficient air for a couple months, if necessary."

"Caleb's right," said William. "The week is based upon twenty people."

Caleb grinned. "And we're five because Nicky doesn't breathe."

"We'll only be here a day, two at max before we blow Nevada and make way for Texas," Brock said.

"A moot point then. How has this bunker stayed off the radar?" William dropped the bag of 2252s he'd carried from the point where they'd separated from Fran's party.

Brock mopped his head. "According to my dad, this bunker was used by a secretive group known as the *Freedom Fighters* back in the early twenty-first century. It was during the country's snafu battling Iran over oil. Most of them were disgruntled vets who believed the country was going to break into factions and be in a constant state of turmoil."

"Visionary and it explains why Mil is ignorant of this location."

Caleb grinned at William's bemused smile. The old man seemed to be tickled he knew something Mil didn't. "How did your father learn about this place?" Caleb asked.

"He saved the life of the leader of the secret society early in his career. In appreciation, he told dad about it. It's one of several throughout the country and is used as a place to hunker down when everything goes to shit. Once they went fully automated, none of the silos were manned. They're interconnected by tunnels. If the worst happens, we go to another silo and raid it of its scrubbers."

"Ah," Caleb grinned. "This time a good deed wasn't punished." As William suddenly leaned into him, Caleb eased his father to the floor. "Is something wrong, Dad?"

Brock glanced over. "He'll be fine after a nap. I pushed his reanimation process from twenty-four hours to four."

He yanked open the last set of doors and pulled out one of twenty small devices and stared at it. "I've seen something like this before, but I can't remember where."

"Put it aside for now," William said. "Nicky can research his memory banks and give us a report."

"You know," Caleb said, "We might not have as much

oxygen as we think. It would appear someone who knew about this place also came here at some point for protection."

Brock sighed. "That's a possibility. Once the girls get here, Nicky can check out the connected silos and bring back a dozen or more scrubbers."

Caleb met his gaze. "I'm not putting Win's life at risk. We'll sleep in shifts." He joined Brock at the storage unit and removed a gun of some kind. "Either of you know what kind of weapon this is?" At their no responses, he sighed, "We'll ask Nicky about that too."

"Speaking of Win and Nicky," William said as he sat on the floor cross-legged, "Where are the women? I thought they had the shorter route."

"Fran did have a twisted ankle," Brock said. "But Nicky was capable of carrying her and losing no time. Unless …"

""Unless, what?" Caleb asked, his stomach twisting in a hard knot at the thought of Win hurt or in danger. "I never should have listened to you and divided our ranks." His hand clenched into a fist. "If you want to live, Doctor Green, pray Win arrives without a bruise."

He watched as the good doctor's eyebrows raise and then his Adam's apple twitch following a hard swallow. "I'm sure they're fine. Knowing Fran they probably improvised." At the sound of a series of knocks rapped on the hatch in the agreed code, Brock's expression eased. He wiped his forehead and exhaled sharply. "See they're here. Nothing to worry about."

Caleb's eyes never his. "You live right, Doc. Hope you stay this lucky. But a word to the wise, don't ever put Win's life on the line again. I protect what's mine."

***

Win sat, resting against the wall of the bunker. "You won't believe the huge screens they have, Caleb. People can talk in real time all over the country. The screens can monitor every place there's one on the wall, all at once, or certain ones selectively."

"The moment I discovered what my wife had done on the QT, I met with the Constitutionalists and began funding them," William said. "We decided to play along and pretend I'd had a change of heart and agreed with her that it was also a good idea at the time."

"Still is," Caleb said, as he shot his father a sarcastic glance and pulled Win closer to him. "But not when Mil controls them." His face hardened as he stared at his father. "I was beginning to wonder where you and Mil disagree on control of the people."

"You're a smart man, William," Brock said, "I don't understand how Mil conned you during your earlier years let alone the later ones."

Fran chuckled as she rewrapped her ankle. "And

you're calling William obtuse?"

"Yes."

Caleb settled beside Win and drew her onto his lap. His lips covered hers in a chaste kiss, his tongue stroked them, begging entry. Biting back a groan, he lifted his head and held her to him. "Women can make a man forget his name. She obviously had a way with Dad's Johnson."

At Brock's flush, Caleb smiled. Nothing like taking a few licks out on the man whom he considered him to be an imbecile.

"What's a Johnson?" Win asked, wide-eyed.

Nicky grinned. "A Johnson is a slang work which refers to—"

"Too much information, Nicky." Fran's eyes were filled with tears of mirth.

Caleb squeezed Win's arm. "I'll explain later, sweetheart." With a grin, he looked over to where the walking encyclopedia stood. "Nicky we need you to look at the device we found. Also take a look at the weapon and explain how we use it."

Nicky turned the device over in his hands and punched a few buttons, then grinned. "It works."

"What is it?" they all asked in unison.

"This is from the early twenty-first century. This particular model was known as an Android Three, nothing like the Nickys farther in the future, and was more commonly known as a Smartphone or, in the general vernacular, a cell phone. This device contacted a satellite." With another grin, he lifted his head and met their gazes. "It doesn't use a frequency that's been monitored by the government in fifty years."

"That's it," Brock said. "Now I know where I saw one, not this brand but another one. One of the Constitutionalists showed one to Dad and me. He said they used it to communicate with other Constitutionalists because Mil and her security forces didn't remember these bands existed."

Nicky turned it back over in his hand. "There's a number on a small taped-on strip back here. I can try it."

He punched the buttons on the front of the device and held it away from him.

Win leaned forward. "How can he hear anyone in that device with it that far away from him?"

Caleb kissed her temple. "He told me he has supersonic hearing. He can hear a pin dropping a mile away if he wants to."

"Yes." Nicky danced a jig as he pointed at the small machine. "We're friendly and mean no harm."

"Oh, for Christ sake." William stood and, striding to the Andro, he jerked the phone out of Nicky's hand and inadvertently pressed a button putting it on speaker. "Hello, this is agent double oh one."

"One minute." The sound of papers shuffling filled the air. "Is this a certain missing husband?"

"Yes. Is this a Constitutionalist?"

"Are you kidding? You're really double oh-one?"

"Yes." He sighed. "And before you ask, no I am not under duress. No, I have not been kidnapped, either."

"It's really him. He's alive. ... Yes, I'm sure."

"We are safe. That's all I can tell you at this moment. Please give me your pass code so I can verify I am indeed in touch with a member of the group."

"One-five-one."

Nicky pressed the speaker button returning the phone to private use.

At William's broad grin, Caleb knew it was, indeed, an ally. "Yes, I recognize the code. Is that you, Raoul? I'm alive and am not a clone or fake William. It's me, Spiderman." He smiled. "It's good to hear your voice too, my old friend. Where are we? Near Hawthorne, but we need to leave and go to another location. Is there somewhere we can meet a few men who will help guard the party?"

"Looks like we have help." Caleb nibbled Win's earlobe. At her gasp he chuckled softly. "Danger turns me on and you always did."

"Caleb," she said in a hushed tone. "We are in public."

He placed a small kiss on her neck. "Isn't it a pity?"

Minutes later, William handed the phone to Nicky. "Secure it and the others until we need them again." He laughed. "What luck. Two men will join us at the Arizona-New Mexico border. Raoul suggested we highjack a water-jet and fry the security devices."

"I'll handle that," Nicky said.

"Nicky, what about the weapon?"

"There are several nine-millimeter semi-automatic Glocks. There's a lot of ammunition. I can teach everyone here how to use it."

"I recommend you all take Nicky up on it." Caleb tipped Win's face to his. "We don't go anywhere unarmed. Can you shoot someone if you have to?"

"Yes."

Fran smiled at her Andro. "Well, big guy. It seems to me you have all the tasks you can manage."

Nicky rolled his eyes and looked in Caleb's and Win's direction. "I told you I was abused. If you ever commission an Andro, remember he needs TLC. Even if his emotions have been deactivated, an Andro can only take so much stress."

Chapter Seven

Win awakened to find her back cuddled by Caleb, his hand on her breast. At his touch, her entire body tingled. Her nipples pebbled beneath his fingers. She squeezed her thighs together, trying to stop the throbbing. As she tried to pull free, his arms tightened and held her tight to him, his warm breath on her neck.

"Going somewhere, love?" He nuzzled her neck, nipped at her ear and massaged her breast.

She twisted and turned in his arms. "I thought you were a gentleman."

"Don't know why. I'm well known as a bastard." He chuckled. "You'll also notice no one questioned me as to why I wanted privacy."

She froze. "They know what you've planned?"

"I sure hope so. I'd hate to be interrupted."

She shivered. "What are you doing?"

"About to kiss you." His lips covered hers.

She was torn, shove him away or clasp him to her. As his tongue teased her mouth open, a strange fire ignited between her legs. Her chest burned with expectation.

She pulled back, wanting to look into his eyes, but couldn't in the total darkness of the bunker. Not that she needed to see him. She knew every detail of his face as if she'd molded him out of pottery beneath her own fingers. Gorgeous dark, chocolate eyes. Dark wavy hair brushed his shoulders. A straight, aristocratic nose that matched his rough-hewn features. Her finger touched the dimple in his left cheek that only showed when he laughed, and he was laughing right now. He rolled her onto her back, one hand held hers over her head and the other traced down the front of her blouse. "What are you doing?" she whispered as her blouse fell open.

He leaned down, his chest pinning her. "Don't be afraid, love."

"But Caleb," she said, struggling under his weight, "we are less than two hundred feet away from the others." Actually, they were in one of the connecting tunnels, but on the other side was Caleb's father.

"True, but we have a steel door between us."

His lips covered hers. Within seconds his tongue stroked hers as she responded, matching him caress for caress, her toes curling. Delightful spasms of fire raced down her neck and pulsed between her breasts.

"We aren't married," she gasped, struggling not to squirm beneath him as his full length rubbed at the apex of her legs. Each movement he made against her matched the thrust of his tongue. Her mind screamed this wasn't right. Her body yelled back, *yes, yes, more*.

"Marriage is a small detail, love, one we can remedy in a flash."

"But—"

"You talk too much." He captured her mouth and swallowed her groan of pleasure.

As he released her arms, one arm wrapped around his neck, the other around the small of his back. Her leg slid over his, holding him to her as lightning sparked along her nerve endings. Surging need exploded in her core, demanding she get as close to him as possible.

Releasing her mouth, his breath came in ragged gulps. Caleb rested his head in the hollow of her neck, pressing small open-mouthed kisses over the sensitive skin then moved down to her exposed chest.

"What are you doing?" she whispered.

"Just a bit of exploring." He cupped and massaged a breast, then pinched a nipple. A second later his mouth closed over her naked breast.

She trembled with an unknown anticipation. The

throbbing between her legs increased. Her jeans were so wet they damped his leg that pressed against her. "Oh Caleb, is having sex even more pleasurable than this?"

"No," he whispered on a groan. "This is just the beginning. Making love is ten times better."

"Then I shall die in your arms," she moaned.

He chuckled. "Please don't, love. I want you alive."

"Caleb?"

"Yes, love?"

"Now that we're alone, can you tell me what a Johnson is?"

His body shook in repressed laughter. "I could, Win. But I'm afraid I'll have to demonstrate."

As he took her mouth in his again, she teased his lips open.

***

Early the next morning, Caleb entered the room with his arm around Win's shoulder, holding her close. If he could, he'd never let her go. He glanced down at her. To think he'd thought he needed to be accepted by society. No, he needed her to be whole. They would marry, even if it meant getting her pregnant. "Morning, everyone."

Nicky stood next to the light panel, lifted his head and smiled. "Morning."

Yawning, Brock stood and shook out his rolled up jacket. "I've had a better night's sleep, but I have to admit

I was out like a light."

"You seem to be chipper this morning, Nicky," Win said.

"Except for the circuits that stayed on for disturbance patrol, all the rest turned off and recharged. I must say I feel so much better informed and very refreshed. Orgasmic, really."

Fran chuckled. "Nicky, I must curb your interphase and vid viewing. Your language is getting a bit too colorful."

Caleb winced. He had forgotten the Andro's supersonic hearing. Although he couldn't prove it, he would bet the little bugger had been well entertained.

As if the same thought occurred to Win, she jerked free of his arm. "I, like you, Nicky, feel refreshed and exhilarated by my sleep. Like Doctor Green, I didn't know what hit me once I lay down."

"You were very quiet. I only heard you groan a few times," Nicky said, beaming.

Caleb shot the Andro a glare. "What's the game plan for today? Because, I've gotta tell you, the sooner we close in on Mil the better."

"The way I see it, the first order of business is for Nicky to find a water jet and disable it." William grabbed his jacket and threw it on. "Thanks to Nicky, last night everyone got his target practice. Make sure you keep your weapons handy."

Caleb joined his father. "I suggest we race to hell down to San Antonio and get a few coins. Once we have funding, we can figure out how to take down Mil."

"Let's not get ahead of ourselves," Brock reminded them. "First the water jet." He turned to Nicky. "Do your memory banks have any information that will help locate one?"

"Do I look like an Airship dealer?" he asked.

Laughing, Fran clapped Nicky on the shoulder. "Just compute how far from here a water jet is most likely to be."

"Why didn't he just say so?" He tapped his chin. "According to probability theory one should be less than an eighth of a mile away. Most residences are located due east. So I suggest we walk in that direction."

Snickering, Fran flashed Brock a smug smile. "Just ask Nicky for information, but be specific."

"Good thing you're close enough to interpret," Brock shot back. "I'm thinking only Nicky and one of us should find the water jet. We can circle back and get them."

"I'm not staying if Caleb goes," Win said. "What if something happens and you don't get back? I wouldn't want to be here without Caleb." She grabbed his arm. "Please."

"I agree with, Win. Nicky should handle it alone.

None of us can show our faces, not with the price Mil's put on us." Caleb tipped her face up. "For the record, after last night, I never want to go through the worry I experienced again. You and I stay together."

She smiled at him, her face shining.

"Damn." William raked his hand through his hair. "Nicky, you're on your own. If caught, wipe your memory. Do you understand me?"

"Yes."

"Steal the water jet and fry the stealth and tracking features. In case anything happens you can use one of those cell phones to contact us then destroy it."

Nicky sighed. "See? Abused again. Oh, the pressure."

An hour later, Win grabbed Brock's arm. "When's Nicky returning? He's been gone over an hour and you said the water jet's only an eighth of a mile away. Could something have happened to him?"

Brock slanted her a glance. "If that one's gone, he's got to find another one. Just chill."

"Chill?"

"Calm down." Caleb hugged her. "You're the woman who marched more than a mile across snow and ice frozen land to give me a piece of my mind that day in Illinois. You are one of the strongest women I know."

"That seems so long ago," she sighed, resting her head on his chest.

He laughed. "It was."

She stared up into his face. "For some of us it seems a mere few days ago. So much has changed, I'm reeling from it."

"Yes, love, it has and I'm glad."

"I'm happy someone's having a good day," Brock said. "I for one am scared shitless a POP officer is going to, well, pop up at any moment."

Brock's cell phone buzzed. "Nicky? … Is it clear? … No POPs in the area? … Good." He pushed the off button and dropped the phone in his shirt pocket.

"What did he say?" Caleb asked.

"Time to leave. He's landing the water jet right now."

***

"Maybe I should go on that restoration show," Nicky said, gloating. "You know, the one where they steal the vintage water jets, restore them and then surprise the owner?"

Win smiled. "Even though I'm not from this time, I doubt the owner would be happy if all his tracking circuits were destroyed."

"It depends," Caleb said, his arm around her. "If the guy wanted to get away from Mil Davis he'd be overjoyed."

"I believe more people feel that way than will admit

it." Brock talked to them from the front seat, facing them with his arm wrapped around the headrest. "I can't wait to see what the Constitutionalists say about the size of their movement."

"It was already quite large five years ago," William told them. "The last time I spoke to Raoul before the bitch drugged me, the guy said they had more than a million followers. And that was just from the U.S. We have followers in other countries as well, hoping for a return to a peaceful and sane government."

"That was five years ago," Brock said. "Things have escalated since then. Your wife has been the perpetrator of some heinous executions and has also instituted a poll tax, for lack of a better word. Every citizen must ante up a set amount per year which is determined by the Primera. You don't pay up, you work in this century's equivalent of a sweat shop."

"My word," Win said. "This country's worse off than it was before the War Between the States."

Caleb stroked her arm. "Yes, my love. Women still don't get to vote. But neither do the men. Plus part of the country isn't just devastated but has ceased to exist."

She shivered, partially in delight from his touch and but also partially from the chilling truth of his words. "Not to even have a say in what happens in the country. It is so wrong."

"You have one fact incorrect, Caleb," Nicky said. "There is a vote. But the outcome always goes in favor of the state."

"That's right." Fran nodded. "We give new meaning to stuffing the ballot boxes."

"Look down there," William said. "We must be close to the Arizona border, because I see the first orange marker Raoul said he'd place. We must be right on schedule too, because he said he couldn't leave them there long."

"What do you take me for?" Nicky asked. "A novice? I'm always on schedule unlike current public water vans. Brace for steep decline and landing."

"Oh my," Win said. "I hope I can stand the excitement."

"After last night," Caleb whispered in her ear, "I am sure this will be anticlimactic.

***

Caleb looked around the Constitutionalist Headquarters. It seemed no matter what the era, he couldn't avoid caves. He found his fortune in the Sierra Madre when he discovered the lost gold. He found his heart in an ice cave. Now he found his future in a cave of freedom fighters.

Raoul slapped William on the back. "Old friend, I am happy to see you and your companions made it safely.

150

What do you think?"

"Ingenious, Raoul," William said. "No one would think to look in an old Anasazi cave."

Caleb scanned the stone walls. "I've heard of these."

"This is not truly a cave." Raoul motioned around them. "It's actually a small crevice in the limestone and houses a simple dwelling built by an ancient people." He smiled. "Unlike what people of your time believed, Caleb, we now know this one was one of the first peace stations of a Neptunian civilization."

William nodded. "Too bad Mil axed more space exploration."

Caleb snorted. "Some things never change. She liked being a big fish in the pond of New York society. Now she's expanded to Earth and if we don't stop her, one day it'll be the universe." He glanced at Win. His poor sweetheart was exhausted and had collapsed onto a cot as soon as they got inside the headquarters. Brock and Fran had also crashed. Even he was flagging. It was a good thing they could rest until dawn and Nicky didn't tire and could handle disturbance patrol alone. "How many of Constitutionalists are there"

Raoul smiled. "Ah, the twenty million dollar question. As best we know close to thirty million world-wide. We discover new unknown allies daily."

William whistled. "You've grown in ranks in five

years."

Raoul grinned. "That we have. We have you to thank, too. Without your support and money, we would have withered away. Your funds have allowed us to save thousands of innocent people from torture."

"Have you figured out how to pierce her armor, yet?" William asked.

"Armor? What the hell are you talking about, *Dad*?"

"Her personal guard and the elite who support her. Son, this world is divided into the haves and have nots."

"It always was."

"Not like now. In the time Mil was awake and I wasn't, she mobilized the wealthy. A few families control the world. The rest are worker bees, drones. Some like our doctors over there," he motioned to Fran and Brock, "are at a higher level but they're still drones."

Caleb heart sank. How had this happened? How had everything gone so wrong? He glanced at Raoul. "What's the plan?"

Raoul grinned. "You two are the answer. Once we let the public know you aren't captives. Once they know and believe it is you who are and fighting for the return of democracy, not even Mil can stop us."

Caleb mouth thinned. "We have to take over communications first. Then we co-opt her forces."

"I must agree with my son. We have to discover a

weak link and enter by that route. We have the army, not the means."

"Yet," Caleb said. "Once we start, expect it to take years. No war has ever been won in days."

"Actually, there was the 'Seven Day War' between Israel and the Arabs," Raoul said with a chuckle.

"We aren't Israel and Mil isn't weak like the Arab states were. And if you think I'm waiting years to marry Win because we're fighting a war, you're nuts."

"No need to delay," Raoul said. "We have preachers in our group. You can be married anytime."

"Great. First things first, I have to retrieve some gold. We need money to bribe Mil's protectors, fund an army …" He glanced at a sleeping Win. "… and support my wife and our children."

William clapped him on the back. "Old-fashioned values. You'll be good for the country."

"Win and I leave tomorrow to recover a few coins."

"I think we need to stick together, son."

"No offense, Dad, but Win's the only one I trust knowing the location of my stashes."

Raoul put a hand on each man's chest and pushed them apart. "He's right, William. Also, your group is too large to travel together. Between the bounty on the docs and the reward on the three of you, the risks outweigh the reward."

"Understood. But that's not why Caleb doesn't want me along. He doesn't trust me."

Caleb met his dad's flint gaze with one of his own. 'I've just met you. I'm still adjusting to all of this." He motioned to their surroundings. "I'm still learning to accept you as my father and that you were innocent of Mom's death. I'm not ready to share my fortune with you. It's enough Win and I've stuck around." Caleb wasn't moved by William's look of shock and soul-deep hurt. Maybe one day he could put aside the pain and sense of failure that consumed him at his inability to save his mom. But not today.

"Caleb's right, William. I suggest a group of us escort all of you as far as Waco. You and your group wait at the Jameson's ranch drop-off point while we head north. Caleb and Win can recover the coins and return for you."

"What about the POPs?" William asked.

"If POPs show up once they've left you, take off for Dallas and work your way back here. You'll find vehicles where you left them. I've never moved them or told anyone about them." He turned and met Caleb's gaze. "If the POPs get you, you're on your own."

Caleb nodded. "That's the chance we'll have to take."

"Are you sure about this, son? You know nothing of this era." At his nod, William said, "You may need help recovering the gold."

"Win and I can handle it. Trust me, it's right where I left it. If it had been discovered, you'd know because gold wouldn't be scarce."

Chapter Eight

"This is so exciting," Win said early the next morning as she held his hand crossing the border into San Antonio. "I feel just like a Pinkerton."

In spite of himself, Caleb chuckled. "Detectives we aren't." He stared down at her flushed face. "And for heaven's sake, stop talking."

"Where are we going anyway?"

"Fran was right. You can't keep quiet." He laughed. "If I told you you'd never believe me." He scanned the countryside. All he had to say was he needed to get close to national land and Raoul pinpointed where he needed to touchdown. "Given the world-wide damage the tidal wave caused, the city is huge compared to the outpost of our day. I expected it has to have grown in over two hundred years, but this sprawling, teeming mass of humanity is a surprise."

"Surprise, Caleb? Try terrifying. How did you manage to hide gold on national land?"

He smiled and winked at her. "When you have money you can do almost anything."

"I suppose that's true, but won't retrieving it in daylight be dangerous?"

He kissed her temple and hugged her close to him. "Maybe. But it's dawn, love, not day. I doubt anyone will be looking for us where I am going."

"And that is?"

He pointed to the sign.

She gasped. "The San Antonio National Cemetery?"

He nodded. "Let's go." He grabbed her hand and tugged her along.

"Why did you bury your money with the dead?"

He grinned. "They're not going to tell anybody."

"Are we digging up a body? Because I have to tell you, Caleb, there are some things I won't do. And desecrating a grave is one of them."

"It isn't in a grave. Disturb a grave and everyone notices. The coins don't take much space. Trust me."

"Caleb, perhaps this isn't the best time to tell you this, but cemeteries give me the willies."

"Win, darling, the dead can't hurt you. Besides, the money is right next to a private who died during the War Between the States. I knew his father. Together, we visited

157

his son's grave just before my friend died."

Minutes later, they arrived at the spot, Win's face white and her hand shaking. "How do we dig it up?"

He shook his head. "Oh, no, no. I didn't want to go to that trouble. We just remove the stone."

"The stone?"

He nodded. "See the unmarked stone next to the other grave? It's a true marker to the gold. Remove it and the hole is there with the gold inside a metal chest."

As she crossed her arms and looked at him like he'd lost his mind, he grinned. "You convey even the slightest emotion without saying a word. So why are you such a chatterbox?"

"I see Fran's talked to you."

"And Nicky."

"Bah." Foot tapping, she pointed to the stone. "That looks like it weighs hundreds of pounds, if not more."

"Not this one. Think of a Chinese box. The stone's on hinges and opens if you know how to spring the lever."

She gasped. "But how did you—"

He rubbed her back. "I told you, if you have enough money, you can do anything."

"Are you sure no one's found it?"

"I hope after we're married you have more faith in me."

"Who said I was marrying you?"

He stared down at her.

"I've decided since we're in the Twenty-second Century, I need to get with the program as Nicky says. I'll be your loving and much doted on pet."

"I don't want a pet. I want you as my wife and mother of our children."

Grinning, she patted his cheek. "We'll talk later."

"Tease." He bent and fingered the stone, finding the ten levers and pushing them aside in a specific sequence. With a grin, he flicked the last one and the stone reared to one side with a creak.

"Oh my," Win said, looking down with guarded interest, her arms crossed tightly next to her waist. "How do you open the chest?"

"The old fashioned way." He flicked the latch up and pulled it back. The gleam of the gold on the rising sun was a sight to behold. He didn't miss her audible gasp of shock. "It looks like liquid sunlight."

"But much easier to grasp." He plucked ten double eagles from the chest. Glancing at the sky, he grimaced. "Let's lock it down and get out of here. According to Raoul, the POPs will be making a circuit through here in fifteen minutes."

"Take an ingot. The group can melt it down into one ounce units."

"Good idea." He tossed her five coins and put the

other five in his jeans pocket. "Those to hide." He pulled an ingot from the chest, set it beside and re-secured the site. "Let's go."

Minutes later they made their way back to the water jet. Caleb slid the gold bar under Win's seat. "Let's go."

"Once we're in the air, call your dad. I have a funny feeling." At his grin and arched eyebrow she sighed. "I told you, I have the sight. Just do it, Caleb, but get us out of here first."

Once in the air, he clipped the phone onto the console between them, punched the one number dial that had been programmed into it and pressed the speaker button.

Nicky answered. "Hello, is this Caleb?"

"Nicky, where's Dad?" Caleb asked.

"Captured," Nicky said in a toneless voice. "Right after Raoul and his group left, this guy showed up and took Fran, Brock and your father as hostages. He said he was a bounty hunter."

"What about the ranch owner?"

"As agreed, he and his family went into town. If you're coming here, be careful. ."

Win gasped, her hand clutching her throat.

"I don't understand. How did the hunter know where to find you and why didn't he take you?"

"A Constitutionalist infiltrator. A turncoat. I have my suspicions but nothing I can prove," Nicky growled.

"You don't have any emotions. What are you doing?"

"Getting angry. No one touches my Fran. As for why I'm here, I got lucky. The moron of a bounty guy said I was just a hunk of machinery and I had no money on my head. Me. An Andro, a model 60-52. Can you believe that?"

"Get ready. We'll be coming in hot." He disconnected the call and his hands tightened in a white-knuckled grip on the steering wheel. Eyes narrowed, Caleb stared straight ahead, unseeing. He refused to lose another parent.

"Caleb, what are we going to do?"

He shook his head. "Get Nicky and rescue my dad."

"What about Fran and Brock?"

"Them, too." He glanced at her. "Why's Nicky exhibiting emotion?"

"Fran said Nicky was different from any Model 60-52 she'd ever met. That he learned by modeling humans. That's why he could pass."

"Great, just when we need a load of circuits that functions logically, we're getting an Andro trying out his human side."

***

Caleb landed and waited for Nicky to climb aboard. Win had been surprised he'd taken to driving the water jet. But as he told her, driving it was easier than handling his adoptive father's plowing team. "Do you have any idea

161

which way the guy went?" he asked, circling the ranch.

"He headed north. As to where he's going, I'm not sure. But he talked to himself a lot. Mutter, mutter, mutter. He was one evermore stupid man."

"Pardon me for being rude," Win said, "But he was smart enough to take three of us hostage."

Nicky rolled his eyes. "He had inside help. It's the only way he found us and accomplished taking us out. Which he did one at a time. On the upside, he didn't know enough to take me, a state of the art Andro 60-52. How smart could he be?"

Caleb chortled. "If I didn't know better my mechanized friend, I'd swear you'd rather have been captured and erased than ignored. Did he say why he didn't take you?"

Nicky snorted. "Like I said earlier, there isn't a bounty on me. On the upside, I can help you find our missing companions. I will admit, I'm worried about my Fran. If he's hurt one hair on her head, he's a dead human."

"Brock said it was against your programming to hurt humans."

"And you believed him? Who do you think hunts and kills the Constitutionalists? Andros. Who do you think we kill? Humans."

"I see." And he did. Nicky was programmed to help humans, but if Fran were hurt all bets were off. Not for

162

the first time he wondered if Nicky were in love with his best friend. Woe to the poor man, whoever he was, who tried to have a real relationship with her, much less make love to or marry her. "Considering the man was as stupid as you said he was, he must've let something slip. Think back. You said he muttered all the time. About what?"

Nicky cocked his head and put his finger to his temple. "He kept saying he'll collect the bounty in Oklahoma City."

"Are you sure?" Caleb smirked at the Andro's expression of frustrated irritation.

"He said they were waiting for him at the nation's regional office there. And he kept saying, 'once I get this bounty those folks in Gainesville won't call me no poor moron again.'" Nicky shook his head. "Fool should be working in the mines. You'd think if he's running around loose, he could speak correctly. Even a Model 42-10 uses better grammar."

"Is there still a Gainesville, Texas?" Win asked.

Nicky shot them a look that said they weren't much above the moron who'd taken his Fran. "It was the home of the largest uprising against the Primera in the forty-four years since she took power. Thousands were taken into custody and shipped to Antarctica."

"Then, there must be a huge group of Constitutionalists living there," Caleb said.

"No." Nicky shook his head. "They wouldn't be there in a million years. Not after so many brothers were shipped out. Strange thing is the uprising didn't have much to do with political differences. They were up in arms because the Primera outlawed gambling and closed down the casino megaplex in Thackerville, Oklahoma. The town folks made most of their money from tourists."

Caleb chuckled. "Nice to see the power of the dollar hasn't changed. People will still turn in their mother if it means a profit."

Win darted him a glance. "Strange words coming from the lips of a man who has millions."

He sighed. "Billions. But I didn't make it to control others or use it for personal gain."

"Bull feathers. You used it to buy my father and get his agreement to our marriage."

Caleb sighed. "Let it go, Win. That was over two hundred years ago."

"I was bought and sold. It was slavery."

"It was marriage. Now I want you because I love you, not because you fill a need. Also, marriage to me keeps you out of Mil's mines and brothels." He arched an eyebrow, daring her to challenge him. "Now my money's going to help take down Mil Davis, our be-knighted Primera."

"I knew you were pure of intent." Win planted a kiss on his cheek and turned to Nicky. "So where, pray tell, is

Gainesville?"

"Due north, at the Oklahoma border."

"Let's check it out," Caleb said. "Then, we'll have to find a lake to refuel."

"Not necessary," Nicky said. "I placed three gallons of water in the cargo hatch before we took off."

***

"Not to sound prosaic, but do we have any food? I haven't eaten since last night and am starving."

"Give me a sec." Slipping his hand into a sealed bag, Nicky withdrew a 2572 and passed it to Win. "I've always fixed them before so I'll guide you through it. Press the top. That'll release the water."

"How much water?"

"Three drops. Now peel off the cover and let light hit it."

Out of the corner of his eye, Caleb watched the flat package expand from a shapeless blob to take on the look of meatloaf, mashed potatoes and green beans. "I'll be damned. Smell's great! How's it taste, Win."

"Hot and good. I keep being surprised by how wonderful they taste."

"Naturally" Nicky said. "They're the 2572s, the best Mil's scientists and chefs can create. Nothing's too good for her mercenary army."

Caleb glance met Win's look of surprise. With a shrug,

165

he said, "If I didn't know better, I'd swear you were annoyed."

"Irritated. We have thousands of humans starving, slaving in her mines, and these things cost a penny to make. Does she share them? No. The poor still go hungry."

"For an unemotional Andro, you've been displaying a lot of emotion," Caleb said.

"I've been watching Fran and learning." Nicky turned sideways in his seat and looked down.

"Fran isn't the most emotional gal I've met."

"She is around me."

Win slapped her hand over her mouth and smothered her snort of laughter.

Nicky tapped her on the shoulder. "I heard that, Win. It isn't nice to laugh, especially when I'm telling the truth. Of course, I'm incapable of lying."

"Even if the truth would cost us or Fran our lives?" Caleb asked.

"Humans." He sighed. "There's the truth and then the truth. I am loyal above all other things."

Caleb snickered. Nicky had crossed the border from cool, logical Andro to messy emotional human sometime back. All it had taken was for Fran to be threatened and stolen from him. "Not to worry, Nicky. We'll get our friends back."

Ten minutes later, Caleb flew over a rotting building on the outskirts of Gainesville just over the Oklahoma border.

"Land. There's a residue of Fran's heat signature in that building." Nicky pointed down to an abandoned casino. "Ah, there are Brock's and William's, too. I need to get inside to see how long ago they were here."

"Because?" Caleb bit back a grin at Nicky's narrowed-eyed, and if he wasn't mistaken, miffed glare.

"Because once inside I can tell how long ago they were here. I'll filter the air for their scent. Smell, like heat, dissipates at a specific rate."

Caleb landed the water jet next to the abandoned casino. The façade had long crumbled to the ground. Small scrub and grasses grew in the cracks of the pavement. Vines crawled over the building surface. Within a few more years, nature would have won and taken back the land. "Are you sure no one's in there?"

Nicky nodded. "My laser radar indicates no human life within two miles."

"Don't drop your vigilance. Recharge after we get them back and are safe from the bounty hunter and the Constitutionalist traitor." Caleb shot him a hard stare. "Start searching your memory banks for that last SOB. None of us will be safe until you've ferreted him out."

Minutes later, the three of them wandered through

167

huge open expanses of machines with screens and bells. "Does all this equipment work?" Caleb asked.

"They're pretty," Win said, touching a bright red machine with five windows in the center. "How are they powered?"

"Wind," Nicky said. "Everything went either solar or wind-powered in 2050."

"Are you powered that way?" Win asked.

"Of course not." Nicky crossed his arms. "I'm made of organic material, polymers, self-healing and replicating crystalline structures and a computer for a brain. I am un-hackable and impervious to an electromagnetic pulse."

Win reached to touch a glowing yellow knob. Nicky clamped his hand around her wrist and jerked it back. "Don't touch anything. This place is a trap for the Constitutionalists. The games are armed with protection plutonic beams."

"I see the kill first, ask questions later mentality hasn't changed," Caleb muttered.

Chapter Nine

"Where do we go from here?" Caleb asked. "Nicky, you say they've been gone for two hours. Do you have any clue where they went?"

Nicky crossed his arms. "I've been running through all my memory bank time files and think I have uncovered the identity of the Constitutionalist traitor. If I'm right, then I have a good idea of their general vicinity."

Win patted his shoulder. "Wonderful. What did you figure out?"

Nicky smiled. "While we were in Waco, the men were playing poker. It's so hard for me to watch humans play that game. They make such stupid mistakes. All they have to do is count cards. How hard can that be?"

"Were they drinking anything alcoholic?" Caleb asked.

"Some, the ones not on watch duty."

"There you go." He slanted a glance at Win. "Although I like my brandy as a nightcap, I never have understood the mindset of one who wants to drink just for the euphoria."

"Not to mention the lack of brain and body function," Win said.

"Well," Nicky said, "during the course of the game, Raoul's second in command kept mentioning a guy named Garth Hood, and kept joking about how he'd always needed the money to restore his hometown of Saint Louis, Oklahoma. Maybe he could win it by playing cards with them."

"He was probably just joking," Caleb said as they climbed into the water jet and they followed suit.

"Perhaps about the card game, but they kept talking about his birthplace." Nicky settled into the front seat. "He's dead serious on getting the money to set up a nice cozy town."

"How far is Saint Louis from Oklahoma City?" Win asked.

"Fifty-nine miles give or take a tenth," Nicky said.

"I don't understand why the guy would get that close and just not go the distance to get his bounty."

"Because," Caleb said, "he's waiting on this Garth Hood guy, if he is in fact the partner."

"Exactly," Nicky said beaming. "You're pretty smart

for a human."

Caleb shook his head at the Ando's superior attitude. He could see how, without proper controls and monitoring, the Andros could literally overthrow human kind. "Well, let's go in that direction and see if you pick up any heat signatures," he said. "Direct me where I'm going."

Moments later they circled a small village, all disheveled homes and one small street that appeared it had once been all there was of a town. "This place doesn't look like it was ever much of anything," Caleb said.

"Even at its largest census it was only two-thousand people," Nicky said. "And that was immediately after Oklahoma City shutdown."

"Shutdown?" Win stared at Nicky with her mouth open. "Nobody can get into this city either?"

"Just government employees and civilians with top secret clearance to work in government facilities."

"Besides this one, how many cities are shut down?" Caleb asked.

"All those with regional offices," he said. "Columbus, Denver, Helena, and Knoxville. They were selected because they weren't too close to the water."

"I'm beginning to really hate this nightmare," Caleb growled.

At Nicky's sudden intake of air, Caleb slowed the

water jet. "Did you see something?"

"Down there," Nicky pointed out the window. "That long brick building. All of them are in there, including the bounty hunter."

"The Garth person," Win said. "He's not there?"

"No, though at some point he has to have been."

"Let's hope to God we can get them out of there before the man shows up," Caleb said. "Then we can worry about trying to take him out. I'll land this thing behind the house across the street."

***

"They're in a school," Win said.

Caleb nodded. "Must have been abandoned for some time."

Nicky nodded. "For ten years. That's when the POPs started making more frequent trips out in this direction. Life can be miserable when they're patrolling. Not much better than the mob gangs in your time. They do the Primera's bidding, but have plenty of time to profit on the side. Payola, kidnapping and sex trade, and of course all the sex they could want either willingly or forcefully."

"I'd say that was worse than our time," Caleb said.

"Perhaps." Nicky's eyes darted around their hiding place. "You were already frozen when the Mexican Mafia started. Let's go, coast is clear."

As they headed for the door of the school, Nicky

barred the way. "School's surrounded by protection beams. We'll have to find the master control."

"Where would it be?" Win asked.

"The shut-off is usually disguised as an everyday item, one permanently affixed that can't blow away in the wicked winds, especially those blowing through Oklahoma," Nicky said. "That way there's no universal location of switch box for hostile forces to find. Seeing as this area is barer than most where the beams are used, I'd say we shouldn't have that much trouble finding it."

Caleb stared at the crumbling foundation of the old school house, slowly rotting away. The tumbleweed had collected next to the doorways and weeds grew in profusion at the back of the property. His eyes surveyed the exterior for the signs of anything that appeared to be capable of weathering the years. "All I see is a school sign, a flag pole and a sentry booth of some sort."

"That last one is where the POP guard would have stood duty. This must have been used as an outpost office. It would be too obvious to have the control in there."

"Let's check the flagpole," Caleb said.

They crossed the street to the tall stainless pole, bolted into a steel housing at the bottom. "I don't see anything that could hide a control," Win said.
Suddenly Caleb grinned. "See the dedication plaque? You remember where we had the money?"

Win nodded with a giggle.

"Anybody feel like telling me the secret?" Nicky asked.

"I could but then I'd have to erase you." Caleb crouched next to the plaque and felt around it. With a smile he popped a lever and the plaque rose up to one side exposing a small compartment with a button.

Nicky shook his head. "You are one of the smartest humans I have ever encountered. In a much different way than my Fran."

"Her intelligence is in the form of education," Caleb said. "Mine is from the school of hard knocks. Okay to push the button?"

He nodded.

Standing, Caleb brushed off his hands. "Let's not waste any time. Let's find my father and the doctors."

"Proceed with caution," Nicky said. "The bounty hunter is in there, though I must say his heat signal appears to be weak."

Win grabbed Caleb's shoulder. As he looked down, she went up on tip-toe and gave him a huge kiss on the mouth. At that moment, all he wanted to do was grab her and give in to the sudden rush of hormones that flooded his body. As she broke the kiss, he stared at her. "What was that for?"

"I was preparing you for battle."

He grinned. "I'll remember to tell you often that I am

getting ready for battle. Let's go."

Minutes later they stood on the main hall of the school. Caleb patted his waistband to make sure the Glock was still safely secured there within a second's grasp as they quickly fanned out down the hall. At the sound of weeping, Caleb saw Nicky's body straighten in alarm and then crouch in stealth position as he inched forward toward a doorway, motioning for them to follow.

As the two joined him, they'd all drawn their pistols holding them to fire any second. Nicky kicked the door open. They stared at Fran, Brock and William all tied and gagged in the center of the room. And on the floor, just a few feet away, was a cowboy. Dead, on the floor, with a laser hole through his head.

***

"Thank God you got here before the POPs," Fran said, rubbing her wrists. "This whole ordeal has been awful, from the barn to the hay rash, to the murder. My stomach's been in my throat since he apprehended us."

"You were in a barn?" Win asked.

Caleb shook his head. "It's obvious, Win. They still have the hay in their hair." He stared at the rope burn, red marks on Fran's wrists as well as those of the two men.

Fran nodded as she brushed her hand self-consciously through her hair. "He stopped at his farm for supplies and locked us up in an enclosed stall. You don't want to be one

175

of three people in those kind of quarters, looking at a horse's ass. Didn't smell very good either."

"I'm just glad we found you quickly. I used my memory bank tapes. Once we were in the building though I discovered where you were right away." Nicky beamed. "Of course the weeping helped."

"That wasn't me," Fran said. "It was Brock."

Brock scowled. "Right. I just wanted to beat somebody up, especially that Garth Hood. Worthless traitor. You only missed him by fifteen minutes, maybe twenty."

"How come we didn't see him leave?" Caleb asked. "This area is wide open."

"He literally disappeared before our eyes," William said. "Even five years ago I don't remember us having that kind of technology."

Nicky slapped his head. "I forgot all about the Quantum Dematerializing Accelerator."

"I'm worried about you," Fran said. "You never forget anything. I'll have to check your circuits."

He waved his hand. "It was the stress, Fran. It just got to me. Now that you're safe, I'll be fine."

"Why didn't we know about this Quantum thing?" Brock asked as he stood. He groaned as he stretched.

Nicky sighed. "Top level secret. I was programmed not to divulge the information unless it was an emergency.

I just forgot I could."

"If it's top level secret," William said, "that means only the Primera, her secret service and a few espionage personnel know of its existence. How did Garth Hood get his hands on one?"

"He must be working for the Primera," Caleb said. "Which means the Constitutionalists probably have at least one more, perhaps many within their ranks. It also means we can't trust the Constitutionalists at this point. But the Primera's ploy to blame your murder on us, William, is now foiled, because she now knows you are, in fact, still alive."

Chapter Ten

"Where are we going?" William asked as they took off in the water jet.

"The Badlands in Kansas," Caleb said. "Raoul says he has a place there not even any of his compadres know exists. He'll join us there this evening and help plan where we can safely go from here." He glanced back at his father. "The man was horrified he led you into danger and says now he owes you his life. Again."

William nodded. "I see. Raoul is an honorable man. I feel sorry for Hood."

"You saved Raoul's life?" Win asked. "That's an admirable deed."

William's lips formed a grim line. "It was part of what I fought about with Mil the day before she drugged me. I had always though it odd she wouldn't let me try to unite the Constitutionalists with our ideas, the ones making sense and not taking away civil liberties. She told me they were renegades, bent and determined to grab control of the U.S. and make it a martial state, run by a group of radical leaders who would rape the land."

"Was she looking in the mirror when she made the comments?" Fran asked. "That sounds like what she did."

"They say people always see the bad traits in others that actually are their own worst transgressions," Win answered.

"Well," William said, "In this case Raoul and the true Constitutionalists only wish to return to a true democracy where the people determine the direction of their government and country. People like my wife, make that ex for all intents and purposes, and this Hood person are the antitheses of that."

"About Hood," Caleb met William's eyes. "Raoul said the man would be dead before the moon rose."

"If Raoul says it will happen I'm sure it will." William rubbed his hand over the rope marks. "I would love to see him do it, or at least have the satisfaction of seeing the man breathe no more and not be salvageable for cryo or cloning. These days, people keep showing back up after you think you finally got rid of them.

"Raoul says he plans to bring you proof."

"I certainly hope it's not the man's head." Fran stared

downward, her forehead creasing. "I'm not into horror flicks."

"Most certainly, it shall not be. Traveling with a dead man's head could be a bit noticeable." Win squirmed in her seat.

"Hell, the Godfather got a whole dead horse in the man's bedroom." Brock grinned.

Caleb looked back at Brock in a rear view monitor. "When did you have anything to do with the Mafia?"

"A vid, ignore him son."

Caleb watched the place of anger play over the man's face as he stared aimlessly out of the window. William Davis was a man with a deep well of emotion, some dark and angry, fueled by five years of anguish and misery, wrought at the hands of his wife. From the way he'd wept when he found out about Caleb's mother, Caleb now believed the same anguish existed before the time of her death. His heart dropped to his stomach as he realized how much his father must have loved his mother.

Staring over at Win, his heart leapt in joy. If the way he felt for Win was any indication of how his father had loved his mom, then he had to hold the man blameless of anything to do with the events that had brought his life to such an abrupt adjustment when he was ten years old. This must be what it felt like to truly forgive. By an awareness of how far greater love was than hate.

Minutes later, they landed the water jet in an indentation in the earth's surface in the middle of a group of rocky formations with deep crevices placed just yards away from grasslands.

"These are the oddest canyons I've ever seen," Win said, staring out the window.

"They were formed by ancient oceans in the center of the country," Nicky told her.

Caleb released the doors. "Get out and walk with caution. The paths are irregular according to Raoul and there are snakes."

"Snakes?" Brock recoiled back into the water jet. "I hate snakes."

"Aw, Brock," Win laughed. "You aren't afraid of something so much smaller than you, are you?"

He nodded. "You betcha. They have fangs and venom."

"Not if you blow off their heads with a pistol." She grinned.

"That's my girl," Caleb said, hugging her tight to him. "Stay close together. Raoul says there's hole in the chalk formation called *the Door* that we can walk through. Then, he said about twenty feet past to your left, he made an opening in the ground that can only be entered if you find," he looked at Win, "you'll love this."

She smiled. "A lever?"

He nodded. "There's a hollowed out room in there. He has it outfitted with cots and solar power."

"Where are the solar collectors?" Nicky asked, peering at the formations as they went.

Caleb chuckled. "That's the best part. It seems they're built into walls themselves, a new non-detectable invention from an old MIT friend who has since ceased."

William smirked. "Probably during the Government Scrimmage for Victory. Also known to the Constitutionalists as the Bloodbath in the Sun.

"There was a civil war already?" Caleb asked.

William nodded. "Not as huge or long as our civil war back in the eighteen-sixties, but thousands still died when Mil gave the order to cut down a rally of Constitutionalists meeting in Missouri. They used hideous weapons of mass destruction, all old ancient weapons that have long been outlawed because of their damage to the environment. Napalm, agent orange, even the newer green virus used in the Religious Uprising for Freedom in the Middle East from 2097 to 2100."

He stared at the ground. "I was gone overseas to secure diplomatic relations with the European Allied Countries and to secretly add funds to the account for freedom. She usurped power saying I was unable to be contacted and ordered an emergency strike. The battle only lasted two days. Before I could get back, it was already into day two. When I called off the strike, few were left and the ground in Missouri will be long coming back."

He glanced at Caleb. "I told Mil that night she had overstepped her bounds and had to leave Chicago, go to our summer home in Nevada. We fought over the Constitutionalists and her plan to execute its leader. That night, she drugged me and you know the rest."

Caleb grabbed his father's shoulder. "I never knew how much pain she'd caused you personally." He hugged Win to his side. "Thank God I have a woman who would never betray me."

Win stretched up and kissed him on the cheek.

***

That night, they all sat ensconced in their hiding place, the lights bright from the solar power. At a sudden movement from the earthen hatch, everyone grabbed their pistols.

A white flag drifted around the door. "It's me, Raoul. You need not shoot me. I promise I am a friend and alone."

William chuckled. "You always did know how to make an entrance."

Caleb watched the two men and knew they'd forged a trusting and treasured relationship in a short time, just a few years. But, that's what war and civil unrest would do. It threw the most unlikely people together in a bond that lasted through their lives, one that transcended time.

"We didn't expect you that early," Caleb told Raoul. "After all, the moon has only been up a short time."

Raoul shrugged. "I do my job quickly and without a waste of energy or time." He smiled broadly. "His body was burned in front of the sign to the government compound in Chicago. But, I have brought proof as I said I would." He held up a square case, about two feet in all dimensions. Opening the latch, he grabbed inside and jerked out a head, its forehead penetrated by a bullet right between the eyes. Blood dripped back into the compartment.

The women both gasped, turning away. Brock was the only one who gagged.

"I just knew it was going to be a head," Fran said. "Damn it."

"Thank you, my friend." William's eyes darted over at his son. "Perhaps you should stow it. I doubt anyone wants to clean up after the doc."

Caleb smiled. "I see you do as you say you will."

Raoul grinned as he placed the head back into the compartment, latched it and began to clean off his fingers with his handkerchief. "Always. And so we plan, my new compadres. Where did you want to go from here?"

William grunted. "I really wanted to go directly to Chicago and take out my ex, as I now call her, the bitch.

However my son was right before in saying we must take out the communications."

Caleb nodded. "My father already told me the central communication network is located due west of Chicago in a government compound known as the Sentinel. Nothing like its original California namesake."

"Aye, yay, yay," Raoul said. "Big plans. We must raise a small force of properly trained men to carry out such a task. We, as one, sitting in this room could never do it. There must be properly elected men of every field, some technical, some mechanical, some just good warriors."

"How long would that take?" Caleb asked.

"Months," Williaml said. "More likely years, at least several."

"I knew it, but was just hoping at least that part could be accomplished faster."

Raoul slapped Caleb's back. He knew the man saw his crestfallen face.

"First we do something else I promised. Then we discuss a way to bring on a small victory, a baby step towards the goal."

"What else did you promise?" Caleb asked.

"A wedding." Raoul's phone went off. He pulled it out of his pocket and spoke into it. "Go ahead." Wrinkles appeared on his forehead, a scowl fell on his mouth. "Where?" he growled into the phone. "The casualties?"

His breath escaped in a hiss. "I see. Who?" One eyebrow raised "You're kidding? One coup my friend amidst tragedy. Keep me informed. I shall be back tomorrow evening. First, there is something I must finish."

Turning off the phone and returning it to his shirt pocket, he stared at them all. "It seems the Primera's struck again. She claims the recent murder in front of the capitol is linked to the most current escape of the terrorists. She also blames tonight's bombing on you as well."

"Bombing?" Caleb asked.

He nodded, his eyes sad, painfully red. "She just blew up San Antonio."

Caleb exhaled sharply. "She thought that's where we were. How did she find out where we planned to travel?"

Raoul shook his head. "I don't know. Perhaps through Hood. It is done and cannot be changed. It is best to try and put it behind us. Remember, from every bad thing comes one good, and so it has for us. It seems one of Mil's inner circle has defected, Frank Morris. She'd asked him to murder her chief of security."

"She is a cannibal," William said, his face beet-red. "Even now she eats those closest to her."

"Fine." Caleb smiled. "Mr. Morris can help us." He grabbed Win's hand. "Tomorrow is our day, my dear. Then we plan to celebrate once again." At everyone's blank faces, he surveyed them, a solemn look still on his face. "I mean we shall rejoice at the plans we make to destroy the reign of the tyrant, Primera."

***

The next evening, Caleb pulled the cork from a bottle of champagne. He gazed at Win, the only one present in their hiding place. Raoul had given them silk sheets as a wedding gift. They were spread over a bed made especially for them in the middle of the room.

"Our wedding was perfect," Win sighed. Despite the shadow of war in our future."

"Shh, my darling. The war does not exist tonight in this room."

"I agree." Win sighed. "Having the wedding at the sight of Castle Rock, I felt like a true princess, I did. And you, my Prince Charming."

Caleb gazed upon his bride, adorned in a lace shawl the Constitutionalist soldiers had presented for her to wear. She was like a ball of fire captured just for him, to warm is heart and bathe him in its glow. "I will never tire of you," he said softly, handing her a glass of champagne. "And I promise I will always say I'm sorry if we argue, for I want you cupped beside me every night."

She stood, putting down her glass. "And I shall kiss you thoroughly, as I will now, and we shall make passionate love before we sleep."

"Every night?" he asked, his eyes, widening.

She nodded.

"I believe that could be too much of a good thing," he replied, his voice suddenly hoarse.

She winked. "I bet I won't be the one who asks that we stop the tradition."

He grabbed her and drew her flush against him. "Well, there is no way I'll be the first to give in."

"Then we have a lot of work to do." She grinned, a devilish spark in her eyes. "Kiss me you big loveable husband."

"Well, wife, if you put it that way." He grabbed her ass and smiled as his mouth descended. "Gladly."

After the Emancipation Wars...

This is the end, but only the beginning of The Cash Chronicles. The Emancipation Wars waged on for another twelve years, but at their end, the Primera was defeated and Caleb Cash was victorious with Winnifred at his side. Book 2 picks up with Wallace Cash's call to action. Will Caleb and Win's son be as courageous in ensuring the freedom of the masses as his parents were?

Full Moon Rising

Chapter One

Projecting the image of his current study text onto the dash of the water/solar hybrid, Wallace Cash studied the molecular structure of antimatter and, multi-tasking, hit Mach 12, a nice smooth cruising speed. Lost in concentrating on the calculations, he glanced up just in time to avoid a streaking solar transport and dropped altitude, almost colliding with the heavy vapor trail of an obviously defective ancient water jet. Honestly, why didn't the POPs take them off the road?

Wallace nosed the bubble downward to the landing pad on the solar-paneled roof of his boyhood home, and grabbing his minoplex interphase, he hopped out to take the shoot down to the main living quarters.

There was nothing like home, sweet home. What he didn't understand was the urgent need for his presence at this very minute, in the middle of his teaching year. It didn't matter really. The fact he was nearly thirty was of no consequence. When Mother called, you came, if you knew what was good for you.

Entering the clear encasement of the shoot pod, Wallace sighed. One of these days he was going to invent a better way to enter a home. Every time he had to zip downward, he left his stomach at least fifty feet behind him. The pod accelerated and shot south, and he grabbed, as he always did, for the back of the chamber, only too aware that at any second he'd be spit out on the carpet in the foyer. As expected, he rolled out onto his mother's ancient Oriental floor covering in a ball right next to Raoul Martinez.

"Aren't you ever going to learn how to land on your feet, son?"

Wallace scrambled to a standing position and stared into the chocolate brown eyes of his father's best friend and ally. The man was here as a constant sentinel these days, ever since his gramps died in the War of Emancipation. "Sorry, I guess I'm not very coordinated. Good thing I don't have to be that agile in my profession."

Wallace studied the man, noticing the grim set of his mouth, only a thin line, and thought it odd. He couldn't remember ever seeing this man upset. Raoul was normally jovial and pleasant, even after coming home from the front lines. Okay, with the exception of when Gramps died. However, to his knowledge no one of great import had died lately. "Is mother okay?"

Raoul nodded. "Physically, yes. She told me to bring you to her as soon as you arrived."

Wallace's gut lurched. Whatever had happened must be grave. Wallace didn't do grave well. That's why he stayed in the protected environment of a bubble-enclosed education campus, EC, as they were commonly known. It suited him perfectly, though, at times, Raoul sneered regarding his choice. The man believed in the old twentieth century view of the brawny outdoorsman. Just to think, as luck would have it, Raoul had a daughter, an only child. Wallace had never met her, but undoubtedly, she was not brawny.

They wound their way down a protected hallway to the private quarters of the Premier and Second Officer of the new Emancipated States of America. They were his parents, though he was hard pressed to say which one really ran the country. Once inside, he saw his mother, red-eyed, but still regal, sitting in her favorite chair. She rose and smiled, her warmth filling the room.

"Wallace, darling. Finally." Striding quickly to his side, she threw her arms around him and hugged him close to her body. "I have needed the strength of your presence for hours. Thank the good Lord you're here."

"Laying it on a bit thick, aren't you, Mother? What's with the melodrama?"

She stepped back and surveyed him. "I have never heard you speak to me that way. That EC has made you cavalier. Shake off the bad manners. I need you and your stamina right now. Things are worse than they have been since just after we defeated the Primera."

"I apologize. I had no idea. Though I don't remember what the wars were like, I do recall the pain you went through, including the loss of your good friends, Doctors Victor and Green."

She nodded. "Catastrophic. Thankfully, Nicky is still here, the darling that he is. Wallace, this is worse than then."

He cocked his head sideways. "How so?"

She grabbed his hands. "Your father." Her hands trembled in his. "Caleb died in Arizona three days ago in battle against the Genetic Right."

His legs buckled. Wallace locked them to keep from collapsing and the room turned in circles. Trembling and tears filling his eyes, he stared blindly at his mother, feeling as if his life had crumbled. "Dad is gone?"

She nodded, biting her lower lip. Tears streamed down her already stained cheeks. "He was trying to negotiate, make them realize that continued experimentation without control would end with mutations and creatures we would be unable to meld into a societal structure. Wild and unknown forces with feelings and reactions far different from our own, needs we could never comprehend and hungers we would only abhor. Being beyond our comprehension, the people would be without true weapons to combat such forces, and we'd be faced with the agonizing reality that in destroying them, we could also realize annihilation of the human race."

"How could it have all gone wrong?" He grasped her hands tightly, needing that bond, yet afraid he might break them if not careful.

"They're still bitter." His mother quivered, an action he had never seen from her. Fear was a word she'd never known.

"What do we do?"

She slipped her hands from his and gripped him at the shoulders. "You have to go to the front lines, fight as necessary. Find a way to arrange for peace talks. You are the analytical one. The Genetic Right is composed primarily of men who are scientists as well as educated theorists, men of high education and intelligence. You are the one of all of us most likely to reach them mind to mind."

She let go of his shoulders and paced. "I never made you go to combat training. Perhaps in retrospect that was short-sighted. I always told Caleb it was for a reason, for the people who would inherit the future would be those who use their wits and brain power to solve crises. I believed you would be best suited to be their leader by emulating those qualities. So, I allowed you to continue spending your days in intellectual pursuit while sharpening the minds of many young up-and-coming scholars. Now it is time to use those skills to inform and enlighten our fringe enemies."

He stuffed his hands in his pockets. "How do I get close enough to have a discussion? It doesn't sound as if Dad could do it, and he had a reputation of being able to always talk his way around even the most difficult obstacle."

She nodded. "That is why you must first learn the art of combat and master the use of weapons and strategic maneuvers."

He smirked. "Mother, you said it yourself; I am a teacher not a fighter."

Her eyes narrowed, and he jumped in spite of himself. Well he knew that determined stare. "You will be both."

"But how?"

Raoul stepped forward. "You will learn from my daughter, Elexia."

***

Wallace grimaced as he rode in a government solar transport like a common soldier. Nicky was next to his

195

side like a nursemaid. The men in the cargo hole chuckled and talked among themselves, elbowing one another and nodding in his direction. He'd become a spectacle, one to ridicule and mock from afar.

He turned to Nicky and tried to whisper—not that it would do any good in these cramped quarters. "It appears no one takes me seriously."

"That is because you have yet to prove your merit."

He bristled at the Andro's words. "I'll have you know I may soon be the inventor of the first efficient and affordable way of producing artificial antimatter. Did you know that in antimatter-matter collisions producing photon emission, the entire rest mass of the particles is converted to kinetic energy and that energy per unit mass is approximately four times the magnitude of the amount of nuclear energy that can be liberated using nuclear fission?"

"Of course." Nicky smiled. "Any good Andro Model 6052 circa 2138 with a 2175 upgrade module knows that."

Wallace ground his teeth. Nobody liked a smartass Andro, except for Mother, of course. "Okay, Andros might know, but human don't." He nodded at the other men. "Those Neanderthals clearly wouldn't. I'll take this one step further." He paused and gave Nicky what he hoped was a superior glare. "Since you are such an authority on antimatter, oh wise manmade brain, you already know artificially created antimatter is not a suitable energy carrier, despite its high energy density, because the process of creating antimatter involves a large amount of wasted energy and is extremely inefficient. Only a small portion of the energy invested in the production of antimatter particles can be retrieved in the manufacturing process."

"Naturally." Nicky crossed his arms and mimicked Wallace's glare.

How irritating! Hunk of skin and machination. But now he had him. Wallace pointed his finger at his animated companion. "Well, not even Andros with recent module upgrades know how to make it efficiently for use in future generations."

Nicky cocked his head sideways. "I just ran all the computations, and you are correct. I don't know because it can't be done."

Wallace grinned. "See? You think it can't, but I can do it. I've figured out a way."

Grinning, Nicky unfolded his arms and flexed his fingers. "Don't tell me you think you can actually operationalize the old Frenzian compound fission splitter utilizing a Plutonium accelerator boosted by a ten power solar adapter?"

Wallace's grin disappeared. "You can't?"

Nicky chuckled. "Doesn't work. They tried it in 2162.

You should have done your research."

For the rest of the trip, Wallace rode in silence, lost in a video demonstration of the Frenzian compound fission splitter, only to glance up when the transport landed on top of a plateau located in the middle of nowhere. Taking a quick look out through his small view window, he saw a tiny band of camouflaged soldiers approaching, all armed with old fashioned laser rifles. "My word, Nicky." He nodded at the troops. "They look like they're extras in an old space western."

Nicky made a noise with his tongue. "Better watch what you say Wally. Those are 'the best that you can be,' as their slogan says."

He laughed. "Maybe *they* need a 2175 upgrade."

"'Never ridicule what you don't understand,' quoted from Caleb Cash at the peace signing, July 24, 2153."

Wallace exhaled sharply. "Okay, I'll reserve my judgment, but please don't call me Wally again, even if you have known me all my life. I'm only months away from my thirtieth birthday and now prefer Wallace."

Nicky shook his head, a look of abject pity on his face. "I'll try but habits are hard to break."

***

Thirty minutes later, Wallace held his sides as he lagged behind the soldiers. His face burning from exertion, and quickly losing all breath control, he stopped for a minute and bent at the waist. Holding his hands to his knees, he cursed his mother silently. What was she thinking?

"She thought you needed to become a man, heard her say those exact words. Besides, there has always been a member of the Davis, slash, Cash, family on the front lines since 2141."

Wallace straightened up and stared at Nicky. "Since when have you learned how to read my mind?"

Nicky smiled. "It isn't mind reading but the precise probability of your brain wave function, calculated by many individually witnessed episodes over the past twenty-nine years, eight months, thirteen days, fifteen hours and….twenty two minutes. Had to wait for the second hand to pass twelve."

"Oh, for crying out loud. How gullible do you think I am?"

Shrugging, Nicky stared downward. "Think what you like, I can tell you what your thought is. In fact, I can predict within an eighty-two percent accuracy what you're most likely to think next." He gasped. "And I can tell you that your mother would never appreciate the curse words you have now thought about me. I am but a loyal servant here to assist you in your transition."

The Andro displayed a variety of facial expressions, and then chuckled. "And no, I do not think you are getting ready to morph into a vampire."

"Sorry, but since you already know what I'm going to say, I suppose there is no reason to even speak." Wallace stomped forward. "How far are these barbarians going to make me walk, anyway?"

"The destination is two miles from the transport. You are halfway there."

"Good." Wallace picked up his step. "I can do this. Which direction?"

Nicky pointed to the pinnacle in front of them.

Wallace leaned back and looked up and the cave opening at the top of the mountain. "We have to go one mile straight up?"

Nicky nodded. "I believe the men have a harness, rope and other safety items for you just in case. Though I think they would have been wiser to suggest you just parachute down."

Wallace grunted. "Thanks for the vote of confidence."

***

Finally arriving on top of the mountain, Wallace's arms and legs throbbing in agony and hands torn and bleeding, he entered the hollowed enclosure with Nicky and walked down a tunnel which tilted downhill and deeper into the core of the stone. "Where are the men going?"

"They said they are to wait outside until instructed to

enter."

"Somebody must scare the shit out of them." He stared at the walls, sheer granite embedded with some natural forming crystals. "How could nature manufacture such a solid mountain and then have this much room open inside?"

"It didn't."

Wallace startled at the female voice, and, as they came to a halt at the curve in the tunnel, he looked down noticing the surface beneath them had leveled. Wallace stared back up at a sudden movement. A woman appeared before them. Slim, medium height around five-six or seven, she had short, sassy black hair and her honey brown eyes were trained on him in amusement. This was Raoul's daughter. The same partial sneer curled her lips.

"My father and his men used explosives and bulldozers to dig this tunnel and install necessary power to it as a headquarters during the Emancipation Wars."

Wallace barely heard her words as he took in her dress, skin tight black pants and a sleeveless camo shirt that molded over her bust. Obviously no bra, for her nipples budded against the fabric, pointed and perky. Her black jacket lay discarded over a chair. Besides the camo, the only thing about this woman that hinted at combat was her pair of boots. And even they were spit-shined. "Impressive."

Her eyes gave him a once-over, stopping briefly just below his waist before coming back to his face. "I'm supposed to make you a soldier?" She laughed, her cheeks turning pink.

Affronted, he stared into her eyes. How dare she assess his better qualities. That was what men did, not women. But what angered him was the fact that, while he'd determined her own attributes had promise for further exploration, apparently she'd decided his had come up wanting.

She shook her head as she crossed her arms and continued to stare at him. "My father gives me more credit than I assumed."

Nicky stepped forward. "Ah, but you have underestimated his merit, for he will soon be the inventor of the first manmade…"

"Can it, Nicky." Wallace stared back at Raoul's daughter. "You have not introduced yourself, but *I* am assuming you're Elexia Alvarez. As you have already surmised, I am Wallace Cash. This is my Andro, Nicky."

She nodded. "I go by Elle. My full name is far too grand for a warrior. On the battlefield names should be short." She chuckled. "Which brings me to yours. I can't call you Wall. That sounds worse."

Nicky stepped forward again. "He does have a nickname which is…"

"Not used anymore." Wallace threw him a searing warning.

"I see." Her dimples deepened. "Which means, I suppose, we'll have to give you a code name." Elle strode to the long table behind them and sat up on the top of it. "Now, what name can I possibly give a man with no physical ability and little common sense?"

"I beg your pardon." Wallace walked closer and stared down at her. "I have not been exerting myself in combat activities but assure you I have all sorts of physical capabilities you are not *yet* aware of." He let his eyes trail down her body, lingering at the hollow between her breasts, then continuing downward until he stopped for a full twenty seconds at her crotch, and slowly drew his eyes the rest of the way down.

"Oh, great, he's a womanizer, too." Her eyes stayed focused and firm but her coloring gave her away. "Out here I am not a woman," she snapped. "I'm a commander and am of neither gender when working."

"Then you need to reconsider your selection of clothing." He smiled. "Especially the top."

Elle self-consciously grabbed for her jacket and threw it on, zipping it past her bust line. "Because you have not been properly indoctrinated I will not have you thrown in the brig. This time. Instead, I will disregard your words and continue. I need a name that signifies your essence and

will personify you in a way recognizable to all the men."
She tapped her chin. "I suppose klutz is a bit demeaning,
even for me."

"How about grunt?" Nicky asked.

"Nicky…"

"Definitions three and four. Number three, slang, *An
infantryman in the U.S. military, especially in the Vietnam War.* If
my memory banks are correct that was a war that occurred
in the twentieth century and in which there were no
winners. That particular definition, however, though
fitting, is not the most appropriate one for our current
needs. Instead, I believe it to be number four, slang, *One
who performs routine or mundane tasks, such of those as an
untrained and inexperienced worker or low wage employee.*"

Wallace gripped the Andro, trying with great effort to
keep from strangling him, not that it would help anything
but to relieve his anger. "Thanks ever so much for offering
your opinion."

Nicky grinned. "I didn't call you by your nickname."

Elle chuckled. "Great going, Nicky. Grunt it is. It
seems to fit. Soon he may even grow a snout."

Wallace gave her his most deprecating smile. "It's so
nice to know I am in the company of such encouraging
and supportive comrades. Now will you cut all the shit and
tell me about the Genetic Right so we can determine how
best to make them see reason and I can get back to the EC

where I belong?"

She placed her hands on her hips. "I am not in the least bit used to being addressed in such a way, but for the sake of the mission at hand I will do as requested except for cutting the proverbial shit as you phrased it."

She took a deep breath and sat back down. "Let's see, the GR is a group of cutthroats out to kill and maim innocent people who stand in the way of what they consider to be the best thing for humanity. They are a misguided mob of highly intelligent and well-meaning incompetents." She paused and looked down her nose at him. "Such as yourself…who believe that by continuing research into the manipulation of cells to genetically create new species that can survive the climate changes and population demands of the world, they are doing a service to mankind."

She jumped up again in agitation and what, apparently, was a need to work off excess energy. "Which in and of itself would be fine if those efforts were controlled and supervised by cool, even minds who would know when to abort an experiment if it were in danger of mutating into a threat to our species. Unfortunately, at the helm of this well-meaning and clueless group is a man with icy black blood coursing through his veins, a man who is left over from the Primera Regime. All he is interested in is tyranny, discord and civil war. Just like we experienced thirty years ago."

"This man is…?

"Devlin Hood. His father was Garth Hood, my father's former comrade and the traitor who worked undercover for the Primera. That man was the bloodthirsty bastard who was beheaded in front of Millicent Davis' official headquarters. Believe me when I say Devlin is just as dangerous. Perhaps more so."

"Well, so much great news. Do we have anything going for us at all?"

She smirked. "A well-trained group of troops minus one pompous and totally inept newcomer."

Wallace bristled. "Everyone learns new skills sometime. I guarantee you don't know everything I do."

She laughed. "Not that I'd want to. I only learned what was important for survival. You somehow missed out on that." Frowning, she shook her head. "I would have thought better of Winnifred Davis. She is a survivalist extraordinaire.

"It's nice to know you approve of someone in my family."

"I can give a compliment when it's warranted. Oh, I forgot to mention, we also have Frank Morris on our side."

"Who is he?"

"He worked for the Primera and defected when Hood

was beheaded. The man had his fill of Millicent's brutally massacring her own staff. He is now our chief strategist, and quite brilliant. We won't see him, but he is conferring with Dad at all times should we need to change strategy."

"Great." Wallace rubbed his hands together. "So when do we get started?"

She shook her head. "*We* don't. *You* get boot camp, but first you can get set up in the barracks."

He chuckled. "You mean there are barracks in this mountain too?"

She shook her head. "Of course not. They're at the base of the mountain underground."

He exhaled. "You mean we have to repel down this damn hill now?"

"Of course not. Follow me."

He and Nicky walked with her over to a mirrored wall. She pushed a button and the panels pulled back, exposing a shoot pod. She smiled. "You didn't think I scaled this son of a bitch every day, did you?"

Wallace scowled as he entered the pod and grabbed for the back of it.

Chapter Two

Groaning and holding his back, Wallace made his way into the barracks and fell onto a cot. So much for taking off his boots. In fact, at the moment, he wasn't sure he could. His arms burned like overstretched rubber bands and his legs were like lead weights. He glanced at the clock on the wall. It had only been three days and he was positive he'd be joining his father before the week was out. According to Elle, this rigorous ordeal was because he was on the seven-day fast track. "I don't have time for you to take a month like everyone else," she'd said. We'll just cram it all in during less time." Translation: she was a masochist.

The bitch made him get up at four-thirty in the morning. Breakfast was finished no later than five-fifteen. He was the only one in basic, but still had to be in *formation* for roll call by five-thirty. What a joke! Then it was back-breaking, incessant exercise and training on combat, artillery and strategy, followed by assisting with the building of another underground bunker. Only the strategy came easy to him, and he thanked his lucky stars for at least one bright spot in his day.

He rolled on the cot to try and find a comfortable position, not that there was one. Elle was not with them for the building activities but had assigned a Corporal. She said she was tending to research and planning. He scoffed. In other words, she didn't feel the need to take the beating of toiling under the hot sun and into the cold air once the sun had set in the desert. Everyone else there spent a good eight-hour day on the work with shifts taking over, but he got twelve. Five-forty a.m. to six p.m. He had a short break of fifteen minutes for lunch.

Rubbing his eyes, Wallace wanted all of this to go away. Nicky had abandoned him completely, only saying he had been instructed to report to admin, whatever that was supposed to mean. How had Elle deployed Nicky while the Andro's charge had been left to all but die?

"Oh my." Nicky walked in and sat down on the cot across from him. "You do look a mess. That sand seems to have blasted you a nice shade of golden brown."

Wallace rolled to one side and winced. "Has anyone ever told you Andros are not supposed to be sarcastic?"

He shook his head. "No, thankfully not, because I so

enjoy doing it. You see, my programmer did give me a bit of humor."

"You don't know how happy that makes me. What have you been up to while I've been drying out like jerky?"

Nicky grinned. "I'm afraid I can't divulge that. It's an SMS secret and classified."

Wallace exhaled sharply and struggled to sit up. "What's SMS anyway?"

"Scientific Maximum Security. In other words, if an unclassified person breaches security, we have to kill him."

"Elle's already working on killing me, never fear." Wallace rolled his eyes. "Nicky, I am the son of the leader of the free world. I think you can tell me."

"Nope, lips zipped. Elle says I am to bring you to her so she can brief you."

"Ah, of all the shitty requests. Can't the woman let me nurse my wounds under a hot shower and then eat something before I pass out until tomorrow?"

"Apparently not." Nicky stood. "Do you need help getting up?"

Wallace glared at him. "I may be sore, but I'm not an invalid."

***

"What took you so long?"

Elle stared at Wallace as if he were a common soldier. As he remembered his code name, he decided he was. "I

210

took a shower before I came. I don't do dust well."

She chuckled. "Get used to it. I suppose you haven't eaten?"

He shook his head.

Grabbing a package on the table, she threw it at him.

Staring at it, he then glanced back at her. "What is it?"

"Hardtack." She grinned. "Tooth dullers, sheet iron, worm castles, molar breakers, or just plain sea biscuits. Take your pick."

He sneered. "These have been around, well, forever. This particular one probably dates back more than a century, if I know you."

Raising her shoulders, she cocked her head. "Do what you want. At least if you eat it, you won't starve while I go over a few things."

Grimacing, he grabbed the package and tore it open, removing the cardboard like crackers from it. He bit and chewed. Crap. These were suitably named, no matter which appellation you used. "What was so important you had to call for me ASAP?"

He turned to see a Native American woman enter, her jet black hair parted in the middle and pulled back tight from her face, braided in long plaits on each side. Her forehead and cheekbones were high, signs of the race. But it was her eyes that held him. They were uncharacteristically green.

"Wallace, this is Kenada." Elle nodded to the woman, her voice lowered in what appeared to be idle-worship. "Kenada is a remarkable woman, a seer whose visions have been accurate almost to perfection."

Whoa boy, now Elle had done it. Wallace grinned. She really was crazy. "No disrespect, Ms. Kenada. I am honored to meet you, but I fail to miss how you can help us in a war."

Kenada smiled, and the tilt of her lips haunted him, for this woman, at this moment, seemed to hold the secrets of all times in her hand.

"It is not a war; it is the tipping point for mankind. Thankfully, I have seen the Coyote Moon. It is an omen of impending peace. But first, we must ensure the human coyote is dead."

Wallace chuckled. "Now we're into astrology. I haven't heard about a coyote moon. Is that similar to the blue moon?"

She shook her head. "Much more rare. The moon rises red above the horizon and then flames blue before breaking into full moonlight. I have only seen it once before—immediately following the Primera's death."

Elle smiled. "Thanks Kenada. My Doubting Thomas right here needs to digest your words. If we need more help, I'll come find you."

The woman bowed regally and then strode out, closing

the door behind her.

Elle held her finger up in the air as she glanced at Wallace. "I'll be right back." She walked outside. Moments later, she was back. "I had to clarify something with her, not anything you need to know."

"That woman seems to be very young to be a sage." Wallace crossed his arms. "She can't be more than forty."

"You think so?" Elle sat down on the corner of her long table. "My father says Kenada was grown when he was small. She claims to be one of the Anasazi. She says she doesn't remember her very early life. Dad says they found her in a cave in the Four Corners. She has always been a wise psychic."

"You know how crazy this all sounds?"

She nodded. "Perhaps so, but I have learned to listen to some folks when their track record is good."

"Well, you can't have called me in here to tell me that."

"True." She scooted back into position. "Kenada told me she had a vision of a terrible threat to mankind emanating in the general vicinity of the GR headquarters, which have been relocated from Arizona to here in New Mexico. She said to look in the heart of the beast. I immediately dispatched scouts. They have identified the location of Devlin's SMS headquarters in the middle of the Genetic Rights compound."

His head turned slowly to Nicky. The Andro stood there, blowing on his knuckles and polishing them on his shirt. "Elle, don't tell me you've…"

"Commander. Address me as you should, soldier."

His eyes narrowed. The woman was insufferable. Clearing his throat, he glared at her but didn't retort in anger. He knew the bitch would absolutely throw him in detention without batting an eyelash. "Pardon me, *Commander*, but pray tell me you didn't send Nicky out as a scout."

She smiled. "I won't if you don't want me to. I will only say that Andros are much stealthier and faster than humans are, as well as far more expendable."

At Nicky's sudden widening eyes, Wallace chuckled to himself. Served the mechanized traitor right.

"Not that I'd ever hear the end if something happened to Nicky." She sighed. "Your mother and my father would have my head and probably sentence me to menial tasks for life."

"Doing what? Being a housewife?" Wallace snickered, then clammed up at her murderous stare.

Nicky relaxed his shoulders. "You do not have to worry, Commander, for I don't intend to be destroyed until I wear out and all my function ceases, which according to specs could be several centuries."

"Of course." Grinning, she turned back to Wallace.

"Now, as I was saying, the SMS building has been located. We don't know the extent of the experiments inside, but we need to get inside and investigate, analyze and determine what needs to be destroyed before it's unleashed on the world."

"We?"

She nodded. "You have a scientific mind. Yours runs more towards quantum physics and chemical manipulation, but still helpful when it comes to some of what might be there."

"Thank you. Glad to see you respect my knowledge. And you are going, why?"

"Because I'm in charge." Her eyes flashed. "Also because I'm a geneticist and research biologist."

He sank into a chair. "You're a scientist?" He squinted at her. Surely she was chiding him. A woman who looked like she did couldn't be that smart. Could she? As he considered it, he realized she had to be fairly astute to have him playing soldier in the middle of the desert and calling her Commander.

Her laughter filled the room. "You're not a chauvinist too, are you? You'll put women's liberation back to the mid-twentieth century. I assure you, however, that though you may be close to discovering how to develop antimatter and travel through time by means of accessing a cosmic string, I can delve into the human genome, examine DNA and discover the missing code that makes mutations occur. Between us both, we can make correct decisions and determine the best way to eliminate dangerous experimentation before it has a chance for implementation."

"What if what we find is too large for us to handle on our own?"

She shrugged. "We'll decide when that becomes a reality. For now, I do not wish to consider it exists."

He sighed. "All right, Scarlett O'Hara."

***

"What is this again?" Devlin squinted down at the small Petri dishes with growing organisms.

"I'll attempt to explain." Ulysses smiled.

Devlin frowned. All these damned highbrows thought he had the brain of a pea. They didn't realize he'd jerked their collective chains to be just where he wanted to be, in power. He let them continue with their idiotic experiments, while he orchestrated the takeover of the country with him at the helm. However, they didn't need to know that until his objective was achieved.

"We believed the human genome was composed of exactly twenty-three pairs of chromosomes and the haploid human genome has a possible twenty-three thousand potential genes that bond in forming into mostly sequencing RNA, or so we thought until recently. We now know there are two pairs of chromosomes that are composed of non-sequencing RNA, what we have termed renegade pairs that can be easily manipulated to change form and mutate at will, even when introduced to non-human genes. The sequencing RNA, however, is crucial in translating to gene expression, so…"

"Okay, more than I want to know." Devlin shook himself out of rigor mortis. These scientific types could out-bore any politician. "Bottom-line it."

The man smirked. "As you wish. We are experimenting to see if the human DNA will accept various genes from different animal species, mutating and bonding with them."

"What have you found out?"

Ulysses smiled. "They seem to be partial to birds. Those are meshing and may have promise for mutating humans into creatures with the ability to fly."

He nodded. "Could be useful." *For Batman.* These guys were out there. For him, it was all about getting to the end. His. He'd better do it soon or else they'd have flying people buzzing overhead. "Anything else?"

The geek chuckled. "Of course. In the cryo lab."

Devlin grabbed another jacket from the coat hook. The cryo lab was frigid. He didn't like anything below seventy. There had been too many harsh winters in Chicago where he grew up. That's why he liked being out in the southwest.

They went inside, Devlin limping as always from his one shorter leg, and shivering as he pulled up the collar on his coat. "Why is to so cold? Even worse than normal."

"Temp was ninety-five outside today. Very unusual, really, for early April. Even here it normally doesn't get that high for at least another month or two. We had to take precautions." He led him back to the lab central station.

A woman stood in the distance.

"Fran, I have someone I want you to meet."

She turned and stared blankly at Ulysses. "Yes, Master?"

Ulysses clapped his hands. "This is Devlin. He's a friend."

She stared at him in the same out-of-body way and bowed. "Nice to meet you. I must now complete my duties." The tall dark-haired woman walked off and back into the control rooms.

"Who was that? She doesn't look like an Andro, but a human being"

Ulysses sat on a stool. "That is a clone. The original woman from whom she was cloned was a scientist who died during the Emancipation Wars. We were fortunate to gather samples of her DNA before she breathed her last breath."

"And?"

"The Freedom Fighters had an Andro, Nicky, who was in love with Fran. We believe he was actually commissioned to serve her. But he had true feelings for her, to the point of distraction, and far beyond the normal bounds for any Andro. The woman, not meaning to, made him do things that weren't programmed and almost caused the downfall of William Davis and the Cash clan."

"Okay, but she acts like she's one shot short of a full load."

Ulysses nodded. "Agreed. Just like the woman, the clone didn't want to comply with anyone's wishes. I had to install an obedience chip. Even now, she has a tendency to run amuck after a few days."

"Do you really think she's worth it? I mean, she could accidentally ruin experimentation. Besides, the wars were over a long time ago."

Ulysses grinned broadly. "Nicky is still active and dangerous, especially now that the real Fran is dead. But he hasn't met the new one. We only have to work out a few bugs."

Devlin slapped him on the back. "Way to go. Get to it."

"Don't you want to see what else I have? It will surprise and delight you."

He smiled. "Enough for now. Surprise me later."

***

Couldn't we have waited until daybreak?" Wallace followed Elle as they inches closer to the compound. "I only got five hours of sleep and I feel like shit."

"Zip it and stop making noise." Crouching, Elle proceeded through the sagebrush, avoiding the cacti and the yucca plants.

"Ow! Something just stuck me."

She exhaled. "What now? The GR might as well come out here and just get us with you in tow. Don't tell me you ran into a cactus? Because if you have needles in your ass, I'm not picking them out."

"No, Commander." Nicky leaned over to examine him. "Yucca baccata, the banana yucca. A common yucca species native to the desert southwest, most known for its succulent fruit which the Paiutes…"

"I don't need a botany lesson, Nicky. So it seems he will live."

"Yes, it just broke the skin."

"Never mind, you two." Wallace knew his voice registered his irritation. "Just go on."

Elle chuckled. "For a moment I thought someone was going to have to kiss the boo-boo."

"Shh." Nicky motioned to them. "There's someone just now coming around the parameter of the SMS building."

"A guard?" Elle froze in her tracks.

He shook his head. "Not sure, but the guy has a limp."

"How can you hear that anyway?" Wallace whispered. "We have to be a three hundred years away from that building."

"You never did appreciate my special abilities. I do have supersonic hearing. Hello!"

"You're both doing a lot of blustering when you know you need to be silent," Elle hissed. "If the guy has a limp, that's probably Devlin himself. Be careful. I swear I believe the man has infrared vision. He never seems to miss a trick."

"Well, this time, he hasn't picked up on us," Nicky said.

Elle turned to him. "How can you tell?"

"He's pissing on the side of the building." Nicky muffled a laugh.

She smiled. "Okay folks, get ready. Nicky tell us when the coast is clear."

He motioned to them and they began to run every few feet, stopping behind what cover they could. Thankfully, the compound gate was now open, probably in anticipation of Devlin leaving. That begged for the question of how they would get out if they were trapped within. Wallace shoved it in the back of his mind, knowing if he asked it the question would fall on deaf ears. At the moment, Elle was a woman who was determined.

Finally reaching the building itself along the back side, Wallace breathed a sigh of relief as Devlin drove off in an all-terrain land hover craft. Those he had no use for nor had he driven one. Flying was so much simpler. Yet, he supposed they made sense out here where getting zapped out of the air could occur. Just as his anxieties lessened, he heard the gates clang shut. Wallace cringed. *Stop worrying about how we get out and focus on our mission.*

Elle tentatively stepped in front of the automatic door opening, but it didn't budge. "Secured," she whispered. "It's in an encrypted vacuum lock."

"Now what?"

"At least we can peak through the windows," Nicky said. He began to step from small portal to small portal. "I believe I may have found their lab," he said, in a hushed tone. "There is a worker in there, a woman, but I can't see her face. Ah, now she's turning." He gasped and his body froze in position.

"Nicky?" Wallace strode to where he was and waved his hand in front of the Andro. Nicky was frozen, not even showing reflex movements. "Elle, there's something wrong with him."

Elle raced to where they were. "Lay him down flat." She checked his wrist and then expertly began to examine behind his ear where his control box was located. Shining a light into it, she groaned. "His power has short-circuited. We'll have to carry him back and I'll get him up and running again."

Wallace's eyes widened. "What could have caused it?"

She shook her head. "I don't know. If I didn't know better, I'd swear it was human shock."

Chapter Three

Perspiration poured off Wallace in buckets. "Man, carrying dead weight across the desert as the sun starts to blaze makes you some kind of tired. At least we got back here in one piece. Thanks for thinking about a service entrance to the compound."

She nodded. "That guard didn't even blink when I told him we had a van waiting to take away a defective Andro. It was like it happened every day."

"Maybe bodies come out regularly. Who knows? They are conducting experiments."

She frowned. "That's a sobering thought. Let's see if I can activate poor Nicky. I swear, his face looks like it's been drained of all blood, but he doesn't have a circulatory system. His body has a coolant flow like in the water jets." She placed a stethoscope on him and suddenly jumped back. "My word, he has a heartbeat!"

"That's impossible."

"Maybe, but it's still there."

He walked over and leaned down. "Does he bleed?"

She pricked his skin and watched. "No, just coolant. It'll repair the hole itself in minutes. But it is clear that Nicky isn't your average Andro. His programmer took liberties with Nicky's assembly. Though he is still mostly machine, he has more qualities that are human than any Model 6052 I've ever examined Any model *period* for that matter."

"Can you fix him?"

She nodded. "I just have to replace a power cell. Go over to the cabinet wall and push button 99 for miscellaneous."

Miscellaneous, eh? I like your filing system."

The drawer popped out with many different cell configurations inside. "What size does he need?"

"A 6052-P should do it."

He pulled out a clear container with a small dot inside. "This little microscopic thing can fix him?"

She shook her head. "To you, that seems inconceivable, but dealing with the nucleus of an atom is clearly common sense."

"Everything in perspective." He closed the drawer and it disappeared into the wall's structure. Carrying it to her, he dropped it in her hand. "How soon will he revive?"

"Not for a few hours. He needs to be fully charged up." She popped in the cell and closed the door behind his ear. "There, Nicky will be fine. As for us, time for a nice 2772."

"If we must." He sighed. "Father used to laugh when he talked about Nicky showing him the first 2572 he ever ate. Being from 1918, he was amazed how the food reconstituted with three drops of water."

She handed him his carbon alloy container. "What did he think of the upgraded food?"

"He said he still preferred the old ones." Wallace swallowed hard. With everything that had transpired since his mother had told him about his dad's death, Wallace had pushed the feelings to the back of his mind. Now, he struggled to hold back tears. "I can't believe my father is really gone. It was hard to imagine, even now."

She nodded. "I'm sure. I don't know what will happen when Dad dies." She glanced over at him, her eyelashes dipping in empathy. "Why have you always called your dad *Father* instead of by a more endearing name?"

"I guess because Mother was always Mother. It didn't seem right to call her counterpart Dad as if I preferred him." He exhaled. "Though I did. Not because I loved her any less, nor do I now. But, we were more alike, Father and me, a bit looser and less *regal*, for lack of a better word.

"Mother always did and still does conduct herself like a queen."

"Maybe, but my gut instinct tells me she'd love to hear you call her Mom."

He stared her in the eyes, self-doubt nagging at his gut. "Think so?"

She nodded. "You're her only son and now the only man left in her life. I absolutely believe what I say is true."

"Next time I see her in person, I'll address her like that and see what she says." He picked up a fork from inside the pack and sampled the meat.

"I wish I could have called my mother Mom."

He swallowed. "You're telling me to do something you didn't?"

Yes, for a good reason. She's gone now. Dad says she died in his arms when I was only three months old. Mom was a fighter, a soldier in the wars. So, you see, I never got to call her anything."

"I see. I didn't know." He put his fork down. "If she died as a soldier, why did Raoul allow you to become one?"

"Inbred I guess. You just can't get the warrior out of our genes." She grinned. "Besides, he couldn't stop me and I had something to prove. These bastards aren't going to win."

At the sound of Nicky groaning, they turned. Wallace

glanced back at her. "You said twenty-four hours, He can't be awake yet."

"I told you he was different than any Model 6052 I'd ever seen."

They walked back to where he'd been laid out and now he was sitting and holding his head.

"I feel terrible. I had this horrible nightmare that..." He stopped and slapped his hand over his mouth, his eyes bulging. His hand shaking as he removed it from his mouth, Nicky stared up at Wallace. "It wasn't a nightmare, was it?"

"What did you see?"

He gulped. "I saw Fran. It was her. I should know."

"It couldn't have been." Elle sat down next to him. "Dr. Victor died, Nicky. Remember?"

A sob escaped his lips. "Of course I do. They killed her, even as I tried to shield her. Those barbarians dragged me away and all I could do was watch as they dragged her body away, giving her no respect. They didn't even pick her up off the floor. I thought I'd be chopped up into metal scraps and body parts, and would have, if not for your father, Wallace, and your grandfather with him. They'd infiltrated the POPs' location and tracked them to where Fran and I were."

Elle nodded at him. "That's what dad said. When they got Nicky back to HQ, he was literally apart at the seams."

He convulsed on the cot. "I had a nervous breakdown. An Andro without a glitch almost glitched out. It got worse before we were back to safety. Wallace and William found me in HQ where the Primera's men took me. As they sneaked me out, I saw the POPs throw Fran's body on the pyre, smelled the stench of burning flesh. My dreams, literally...went up...in smoke." He sobbed again. "When I saw her again today, I just couldn't..."

"She must be an Andro," Wallace said. "If it really looked like her, that's the only logical explanation. You know she died. It's also normal, even if you are an Andro, to hope it was really her just like she was then."

He nodded, still shaking. "Perhaps, but I have distance to eye identification. It verified. It would never have done that with an Andro."

The truth dawned on Wallace. "Maybe she's a..."

"An hallucination, Nicky," Elle said. "You've been under a lot of strain since short-circuiting. Just rest and let the power cell fully charge. We're going to deliberate in a strategy session."

The Andro nodded at Elle's suggestion and laid back down, still sobbing.

They walked to the door and out of the room. Striding up to the outside pod shoot, Wallace glanced over at her. "It was a clone of Fran, wasn't it?"

She nodded. "Most likely. I'm amazed they gathered

DNA in the middle of a battle, but I wouldn't put anything past Mil's secret inner circle back then."

"Where were Nicky and Fran when all this happened?"

She sighed. "In a cabin near the battle zone. Your father and grandfather, even Brock Green had banded into a team to try to breech security. Green lost his life there. The only reason Fran and Nicky were left in the cabin was because Fran had a leg injury. Nicky stayed to help her. He helped her all right. They had sex."

Wallace froze. "Hold on. This is not the version I know. All I heard was the POPs nabbed Fran and killed her. A human had sex with an Andro?"

"That's what Dad said." She shrugged. "Nicky was built for it. They'd grown very close. Nicky was in love with her. Besides, he isn't…"

"The average Model 6052. Got it. Obviously. I've always heard danger made you horny, but I'm amazed."

Elle's head snapped back to meet his eyes. "And I'm amazed you just said that."

"Why?" His lips turned up in a satisfied smile. The woman had taken him for a stuck up prude. Not in the slightest. He had a reputation for leaving them wanting.

"Just surprised."

He leaned over, his lips almost touching her ear. "Put me in danger and see what I do."

At her sharp intake of breath and her quick retreat from standing next to him, he smiled.

***

Alarms went off. The sound of running feet slapped on the concrete floor in a staccato beat. Wallace opened one eye and groaned. Staring at the illuminated dial on his watch he read three o'clock. *Damned drill. I'm not going.* He threw the pillow back over his head.

"Get up soldier, move it."

Wallace rolled over as the pillow lifted from his head and slammed into the wall below him. He squinted at the Corporal's face shadowed in the flashing red lights. "Why do you guys have to torture us with a drill when we only have an hour and a half, two at the most to sleep?"

"This isn't a drill, lard ass. Get out or you'll be sorry."

Wallace scrambled out of the bunk. "I already am. Who could be attacking us?"

"Intel reports GR forces. Get outside."

The Corporal was gone the minute he said the words, as was everyone else. Wallace struggled with his boots. He'd be left in the dust while the troops scrambled across the nighttime desert sand. Not a very appealing thought. He rushed to tie the last lace before grabbing his knapsack. You'd think after this many centuries someone would have thought of a better way to carry a soldier's gear. He guessed it wasn't the time to ponder the absurdity of that.

Exiting the bunker, Wallace stared at the night sky. Nothing hinted at danger but the soldiers running away from him. How had the information of the attack been communicated anyway? It had to be a false warning, nothing to get worked up over. He exhaled. With his luck this was a vision conjured up by Kenada. Like the woman could really see the future.

As he crested the hill, he saw the men in the distance. At a sudden rustling in the brush behind him, he turned and looked to see what it was. Elle was supporting Nicky on one shoulder and dragging him across the ground.

"I thought he was okay last night."

"Relapse. I couldn't leave him behind."

"I can do that." Wallace reached for the Andro and froze at the thundering sound of engines overhead. Staring up again into the starlit sky, he saw approaching war jets. Still standing stock still, he watched in horror as lights shone down on the desert floor below them and centered on the troops. A laser shot down, exploding. As the ground rocked beneath his feet, he grabbed Nicky and lowered him to the ground. Crouching there, he stared in shocked silence. Bodies lay strewn across the sand. A shrill piercing noise followed and a close target trans-molecular aggravator hit ground zero, incinerating the remains. The acrid odor of burned flesh permeated the air.

A sob of anguish escaped his lips as Wallace struggled to hold back tears. He never cried but had been on the verge twice in twenty-four hours. Still, there was no way to escape the feeling. It was one thing to see war on an interphase and something entirely different to see, hear and smell destruction. His body shook with its reality. Fear, anger, overwhelming sadness warred for supremacy.

"Stay where you are, Wallace," Elle whispered. "I don't think they know we're here. It's best if we sleep in the brush until we know they've left for the night. Then we can get the hell out."

"Do you think they'll check headquarters?"

She cocked her head. "Interesting thought. The soldiers are definitely all gone."

As she said it, the sound of thundering war jets flew overhead. They ducked their heads, camouflaging their bodies against the sage. Once again, a sound pierced the air as an aggravator dropped from the ships. He held his hands over his ears as the high-pitched screech grew even louder, vibrating through his body. Rocks slammed into him. Dust hung over him in a thick cloud, invading his mouth and burning his eyes. He coughed as he struggled to breathe.

"So much for headquarters," Elle screamed, then sneezed repeatedly, against the sound of retreating war jets. "Hope you like to sleep on a flat surface."

***

Wallace woke up, cramped, sore and cranky. Sleeping on the ground wasn't ideal for sleep, but when you're dead tired it worked. He felt a heavy weight on his stomach and looked down to see Elle's head resting on it. She must have moved sideways in her sleep, obviously seeking a more comfortable position. Who'd have thought that position would be resting on him?

He glanced around to find Nicky, but saw no sign of the Andro. Where the hell did he go? Wallace sniffed the air and smelled the aroma of fresh meat wafting past him. Where was that coming from? He rose up on one elbow and Elle's head clunked to the ground. She sat up in a nanosecond.

"What's going on?" Her eyes widened and then narrowed as she let out a low moan. "Oh shit. We are here. I was hoping it all wasn't real."

"Afraid it is, but I smell something cooking and Nicky is nowhere to be found." She moved, cursing under her breath as she did, and Wallace grinned. The woman was a true soldier.

"Geeze, you'd think he'd have stayed put after all the trouble we went to in getting him out of there safely. Dad better thank me for this later."

"Don't give me that. You'd have done it anyway."

"Yeah, maybe." She eased up into a sitting position.

"Was I lying on top of you?"

He chuckled. "In a manner of speaking. It doesn't matter. I think we better find out where Nicky went."

"Here I am." Nicky walked out from the overgrown brush, carrying long stick with a smoking piece of succulent meat pierced on one end. "Just making breakfast." He grinned. "Grilled rabbit."

"Jack rabbit?" Wallace scoffed. "Probably be as tough as shoe leather."

"If you'd rather starve, fine." Elle frowned. "It smells divine. Thanks, Nicky. You must be feeling better."

He nodded. "Yes, though I had the oddest dreams."

"Since when does an Andro dream?" Wallace silenced when he met Elle's stare. "Okay, I give up. He's special. Yeah, got it."

Elle took the rabbit from Nicky and set it on a rock to the side of where they slept. Drawing her knife out of its sheath where she'd laid it the night before, she whacked it down on the carcass, severing off a piece. "Not exactly like carving the Thanksgiving bird, but effective." She handed the knife to Wallace.

He sat there transfixed. "Remind me never to get you really mad." He sliced into the remaining rabbit and peeled off some meat.

"Better take less time with all actions out here, Wallace. Time will be of the essence to stay ahead of

235

Devlin's head hunters. He must have gotten word someone was in the camp, and the man's no dummy. He knows what he's doing and will make sure he killed us too, even if it takes a few days for him to decide the dirty deed is done." She chewed a piece of meat and made a face. "You're right, not filet mignon. But, Nicky has made it edible. Thanks."

Nicky bowed. "I owe it to you. Otherwise, I'd be in a compactor right now. I suppose I am the cause of those men getting killed." He stared at the ground and crossed his hands.

She shook her head. "Not really. It would have happened one way or the other. The fact is we could have been trapped inside the compound. Your prone body actually acted well as a ploy to get us out. So don't feel guilty. Right now, we just have to consider how to get to Dad's bunker safely and then determine how best to fight the GR."

Swallowing, Wallace leaned back on one elbow. "Mother sent me here to talk to the scientists. How can I get to them without Devlin interfering?"

"Don't know right now, but it's a great question for Kenada."

"Now she's a strategist?"

Elle turned, her eyes narrow and penetrating. "Have a better idea?"

"Guess not. Carry on, Commander."

Two hours later, both Wallace and Elle panting, they paused for a water break. "How much farther is it to the bunker?"

"Don't know. Dad said it was half a day's walk. He was a hard core soldier of many years and was used to marching through extreme conditions. For us, it may take longer."

"What encouraging news." He wiped the beads of perspiration from his forehead.

"I am most stressed that the two of you do not have an adequate cooling system." Nicky's paced around them.

"Don't rub it in." Elle stared at her compass. "We're on track with his detailed map of the location. I don't dare use GPS. It'll get picked up in a split second. We can't take that chance."

"Can they monitor the chip inside it?" Nicky asked.

"Shit!" Elle grabbed it out of her pocket and handed it to Nicky. "Get the damned thing out of there and destroy it."

With great skill, Nicky tore off the outer covering and carefully removed a small cylindrical object, about the a quarter the size of a flattened pea. He placed it on the ground and stepped on it, grinding it into the earth. "There. It doesn't work anymore."

"Have you figured out where Kenada is going to be,

next to some river that doesn't run?" Wallace took another sip from his canteen.

"Maybe the Animas. This time of year, the river gets very low, in spots dry. Too bad. They say it once had plenty of water."

"Yeah, well natural resources dwindled during the Primera's reign. Mother is working on some conservation projects that should help bolster things."

"I hope so." She mopped the sides of her head. "We should be close to the Aztec ruins. The Animas isn't far from them. Maybe Kenada will be there. Let's hope so. She can help us."

At a shrill ring, Elle jumped. "What is that?"

Wallace cleared his throat. My interphase. Don't worry. It's been specially equipped with Mother's government non-detection feature. Devlin can't access the frequency." He pulled it out and pushed a button. His mother's face wavered before him in the heat of the day. "Hi, Mother. Sorry for my appearance."

"Darling, you always look good to me. I'm happy to see Elle's roughed you up a bit. However, I am not happy to hear reports of downed troops near your approximate location. Were they bombed?"

"Yes. Last night. We're headed for a secure location."

"I see." She sighed. "I hate to tell you this, but the Genetic Right has sealed off the New Mexico border and their leaders have issued instructions to me that I must comply with their wishes or you will die."

He closed his eyes. "Why am I not surprised? I'm assuming you said no."

"Of course. I will not stand idly by and sign away the country's rights to free experimentation, nor lift the trade embargo with other countries for transport and trade of mutant species. Please be careful. Raoul says he has planted aides close by. He says they will not appear to be as you envisioned them to be, so keep your mind open."

"That's an odd thing for Dad to say," Elle said, peaking around Wallace's shoulder.

"Hello dear. Nice to see you but sorry it is under such stressful circumstances. As for your father, I am very accustomed to his somewhat different approaches to warfare. You haven't seen them as I have. Stay close and be careful, children."

Her face faded from the screen.

Wallace started to put the interphase back in his pocket.

"Grunt?"

"Yes, Commander?"

"Does the encrypted interphase have GPS?"

He ground his teeth. "Forgot about that."

***

Two grueling hours later, they saw Kenada standing in

the distance waving. "There she is." Elle waved back. "The woman has erected a tent out here. How in heaven's name did she do that by herself and get this far ahead of us to boot?"

"Well, a woman who is from the time of the Anasazi has to be a bit magical, don't you think?" His eyes widened, looking like an innocent schoolboy. "Why do you think I'm kidding? If you can believe in one, you certainly should believe in the other."

"She is obviously from the future." Nicky nodded emphatically.

Elle blinked. "How did you come up with that conclusion? She says she's from the past."

He shook his head. "No, she said she was an Anasazi. They were from the future."

"How would you know?" Wallace grinned. "You may be older than we are, but you're not that old."

He shrugged. "Theorists have speculated that these people, who came from nowhere and during the thirteenth century, at the height of their success, seemingly disappeared into nothingness, actually were visitors from another planet. We originally thought they were from a Neptunian colony but now known the Anasazi caves were not. From my own perusal of the literature in my memory banks and what we now know regarding the possibility of time travel, it is quite possible these were people from the future who planned on colonizing the US before their home orb was destroyed. Unfortunately, it appears they were preyed upon by a segment of a primitive warring nomad group, because there was evidence of a lot of cannibalism. Thus, the majority of the Anasazi settled in the high caves to ward off further attacks."

Wallace clapped. "Well thank you Professor Nicky for your hypothesis. We'll have to ask Kenada."

Minutes later, Elle collapsed on the dirt next to Kenada's tent. "How did you get here so fast?"

The woman stayed seated Indian-style, her legs crossed and feet propped up on them. "I knew a shortcut."

"Well, you can't argue with that one." Wallace sat down next to Elle. "Kenada, Nicky was just telling us a bit about the Anasazi. Where did they come from anyway?

A hint of a smile crossed her lips. "No one knows where we're going and no one knows where we've been. We come where the wind directs us and go where the times demand."

Wallace turned to Elle. "I think I like Nicky's conclusion better."

Elle shoved him. "Don't listen to Wallace, Kenada, he's full of shit. We're trying to get to dad's bunker. How far away are we? If I had the directions right, it should be close."

She nodded. "It is right over the next hill."

"If you were this close, why didn't you make shelter underground?"

The woman crossed her arms. "I do not enter another's dwelling without permission."

"Well of all the…"

"Courteous things to do," Elle said, interrupting Wallace. "You have permission. Dad said there are three separate areas available to us, all dug by hand through the hard effort of his men at the beginning of the Emancipation Wars."

Kenada bowed her head. "My thanks, Elle. We need to seek cover soon. The scouts for Hood are searching. I know they will soon be in our area. Time is precious."

"Agreed." She grunted as she stood. "Let's do it now before all my muscles lock up."

Kenada popped back on her feet as light as a feather.

Nicky elbowed Elle and winked. "From the future."

Chapter Four

The lights blinked inside the bunker and Wallace shook his head. "These old solar paneled lights need upgrades. With the amount of sunlight out there today, they should be working fine."

"The solar rays may have been interrupted by a heat-seeking satellite scan." Nicky went back to using his thumbs on a game.

"True." Elle sat in one of the molded chairs at the table. 'Devlin's looking for us. He's going to use all the technology he has. Some of it we may not even know about yet. The men he's duping are geniuses in their respective fields."

"Well, I'm just glad the Primera's not around to be the ringleader." He leaned back against a dirt wall. Mom says the woman was as close to a devil as she's ever met then or since."

"She was the devil." Nicky's jaw jutted. "She killed my Fran. After what happened in the compound, it's obvious that I'm suffering from PTSD."

Wallace shook his head. "Come on Nicky, you're a…"

"Very sensitive Andro." Elle threw him a murderous glare.

Her finishing his sentences was beginning to get on his nerves. Why did she protect Nicky so much anyway? Oh well, he guess he could comfort as well. "Your past is very important to you. Try to remember them as memories you will always have."

He nodded. "I know. I'm trying. It's just hard to forget what the Primera did to us."

"It's not over yet." Kenada stared off into space.

Wallace cleared his throat. "Look, I know you're psychic, but can you give us some good news?"

She turned to him, her eyes intent on his. "I have, the Coyote Moon. For in the past, the coyote and the owl came upon the Kachinas, the keepers of the moon and sun. The coyote was bent on stealing the moon for its light. But the Kachinas tried to protect it. While they were asleep, the coyote stole the light and it slipped away to shine in the sky."

He saw her eyes crease, and she chuckled. She'd seen his annoyed look. Good. These were Native American legends and nothing more.

Kenada stood. "Now the coyote howls its anger at the nighttime sky. But, they know that there will be two keepers of the light, kindred spirits, ones who differ as day and night. These two shall join as one and, through their union, they will possess the force to kill the human coyote forever and free the moon to spread its beauty over a peaceful world."

"Forever?" Elle asked.

"I didn't say forever. But for now."

Wallace leaned to the right on his elbow. "I suppose now you're going to tell us that Elle and I are the keepers."

Kenada's grin widened. "You are smarter than I thought."

"Now wait!" Wallace sat up straight.

Kenada held out her palm. "Do not argue, but heed the words I have spoken. I will circle around our site and listen to the wind for enemies. When and if I come back before daybreak, I shall rest in the quarters next to the opening." She strode to the door and walked out.

He turned to Elle. "Do you believe what she said?"

Nicky stood. "It's getting late. I'll take Bunker three and you guys stay here. I'll be playing with the interphase until morning. Yes, I will recharge it before we leave." Quickly he made his way outside, shutting the door once again.

Elle laughed. "It seems Nicky didn't want to be in the

line of fire."

"You don't think we're keepers of the light, do you?"

She nodded. "If Kenada said so."

He scooted forward on his bunk. "Come on, there's no way we could join in anything but survival."

She cocked her head sideways. "Oh, I don't know about that, but I do know Kenada doesn't make mistakes. I told you she was virtually free from error."

"See?" he laughed as he pointed at her. "Virtually is different than always, smart shit."

"What happened to Commander?"

"That went out the window along with boot camp, hot desert and talk of stealing the moon. I have to admit your boobs had me going there for a while. And frankly, your crotch was, well, very accessible when we first met. But, now I realize what a hard ass you really are, a real suffragette in a whole new century."

She smiled. "You ought to like that. Your mother was one."

"I don't want to have sex with my mother. Are we talking Oedipus complex or what?"

Laughing she walked over to him and sat down. She leaned over with her lips close to his ear, her breath blowing on it. "I don't want to have sex with your mother, either."

That was enough of an invitation. He was, after all, a

red-blooded American male. Wallace turned and began to tug her shirt out of her pants.

She pushed her hand on his chest. "Whoa Rover. Ground rules. I made the first move because I'm horny. Understood? No more comments about what we do in here tomorrow. None. This is not about love-everlasting or happily-ever-after. I am not going to play Jane to your Tarzan. This is about my need to get laid. Got it? If we need to kill the coyote, we do it, but afterwards, you go your way and I go mine."

He backed off. "I am not the naïve woman and don't like being treated like one. I didn't think I had to spell out ground rules."

Her eyes narrowed. "You needed to hear mine. You're hot okay? Puff out your chest. It appears you're also hung. Great quality in a sex partner. I don't want attachments or stereotypes. My mother lost her mojo when she got soft. Not me."

He kneaded the back of his neck. "You're scaring me. You're almost feral. How about we have sex? That's all I want. Just promise not to go for the jugular."

She climbed up onto the bed and advanced on him. "Just let me take the lead, all right?"

"Okay." He beamed and placed his hands behind his head. "Take off my clothes boss lady."

"The lead. I didn't say you just lie there. Do your part,

or I'll boot you over with Nicky."

He leaned forward and pushed her back into the mattress. "Just what I thought. You're all bark and no bite." He got up on his knees and placed one on each side of her, pinning her arms down and staring into her melting white-hot caramel eyes. "There's no way this night is going to be one-sided."

She smiled as he pulled her tank off over her head and bent his head to her nipple. "Oh yeah. No question about that. You have a talented tongue soldier."

He looked up and grinned. "Wait until you get a load at what my cock can do."

"Take your time." She sighed. "I want to enjoy the ride. But I want to get that load at the end."

"Then you might have to cut it short and we'll go back for the ride."

"I can do that too."

He unzipped her pants and looked down. No underwear. "Commando, eh?"

She grinned, her lids now partially closed. "I am the Commander."

"Not now. Lift your ass."

She did as he asked, and he shimmied the pants down and off her feet with her willingly lifting them from the mattress. "When are you going to get rid of all of yours?"

He popped the button off his shirt as he moved

quickly to remove it. "Don't guess you have any thread with you? Oh well, it isn't needed anyway. Not for now."

He got up reluctantly from straddling her long enough to remove his pants and jockeys which he did have on and scrambled back into his previous position. "Now where were we?"

She raised up on her knees and pushed him back on the mattress. "At the point where I took over." She crawled on top of him and he let her willingly. "If someone's going to suckle, stroke and go down, I'll do it first."

He grinned. "I will gladly let you have your way."

"But I get it back."

"Of course. It seems only right."

She closed in on his cock and her mouth took it all. He raised up to meet her and moaned low as her lips closed around the shaft. "Who the hell taught you to do that?"

She didn't answer. She was busy, but as she let up and began to lick him, he decided he liked women's lib. In fact, he loved it. But that was enough of this, because he had to drive inside her, feel her muscles clutch him and hear her scream for more. He rose up on his elbows and knocked her over. "Okay I liked it. Now get ready for the whole enchilada."

She laughed as he pushed her back into the sheets.

"How do you know I'm ready?"

"I'm willing to bet you're slicker than a greased oil pit on a hundred degree day."

"Not very romantic, Wallace."

"That comes later." He drove into her and delighted in her wonderful lubrication.

"Oh wow." She surged up to meet him, digging her fingers into his arms. No need to talk any more. He pumped inside as she arched to give them both full release. She was so hot, the juices sluicing in and out of her as their bodies made forceful contact. This was all about need, overwhelming desire and lust. Far from a love tryst, this was about sexual satisfaction, yet he wasn't sure he could ever get enough of her distinctive brand.

Chapter Five

"Good morning everyone." Nicky grinned as Elle let him in the bunker room the next morning. "My, my, did you hear that underground rumble last night?"

Wallace stared at him. "I was sound asleep. Slept like a baby."

Nicky chuckled. "Well, you know my supersonic hearing. Got an earful. Guess you were deep into…sleep." Seeing Wallace's headshaking, he turned to Elle. "I have gone looking for Kenada, but she hasn't returned yet."

A rap sounded out the signal on the door and Nicky's eyes widened. "Now *her* footsteps I didn't detect."

Elle opened it. "Kenada, did you get some sleep?"

She smiled. "Of course. Time is but a spiral with many outlets for rest."

"I'm not sure I can handle a riddle this early." Wallace walked to the table and grabbed a reconstituted nutrition snack. "I wish you'd nabbed some wild game on your way back here."

"I wouldn't eat the game in this desert." Kenada shook her head. "Contaminated with chemicals from the GR experimental lab."

Wallace's stomach lurched as he turned to Nicky. The Andro held up both arms in surrender. "How was I to know? I just thought the rabbit had an extra leg by a fluke."

"One meal will not harm you, but you are better off with as little as possible." Kenada held out her hands. "I have brought you some manna."

"What is it?" Elle walked over and examined the sack of round cakes.

"A gift from beyond for your trip across the desert. I made them from the raw dew."

Elle lifted one out and tasted it. "This is great. It tastes like honey."

"Let me try one." Wallace got up and strode over to Kenada's open sack. Taking one out he bit into it. "Oh yeah, much better than that sawdust bar."

"It is good medicine for the eyes." Her eyes sparkled. "And your stamina for the trip and afterwards."

"Great." He diverted his eyes from the woman's all-knowing stare. "Any sign of the enemy?"

She shook her head. "Most likely they have regrouped

at the border. I would suggest you do the unexpected and head back to their compound."

"No way can we do anything inside. It's a trap." Wallace crossed his arms. "We just barely got out the last time."

"There are allies there." Kenada nodded knowingly. "Two of them."

"How do you know this?" Elle strode to the cabinet and removed a container of water. Popping the pressurized top, she took a gulp. "Certainly you didn't enter their headquarters, did you?"

She shook her head. "I simply know. Both are not as you would expect, but where they can do most good."

Elle smiled. "They must be the aid my dad alluded to. He's right, I would never have supposed they would have been in the compound. Okay, Kenada, we're on our way."

As they packed up, Wallace stared at the woman, who finally had taken a seat. "Aren't you going too?"

She shook her head. "I will stay here."

"Now wait a minute…"

"It is as it should be. No need to fear."

"Good enough for me," Nicky said.

"It would be." Wallace exhaled sharply. "You can't die unless they chop you into spare parts. But, I guess I have no choice. It's apparently what we must do."

"Get your ass in gear soldier." Elle stood straight.

"Time to move." As she turned he whacked her on the butt.

She twirled around and glared at him. "Why did you just do that?"

"You told me to get my ass in gear." He winked at her.

"It's not yours, and you'd be in detention for that if we weren't where we are."

"That would be okay as long as you'd agree to come with me."

She turned, ignoring his comment.

Nicky slapped his knee. "Yep. Slept like a baby."

***

"Where could they have gone to? The desert is wide open. They must be hiding in a cave." Devlin scowled. "Damned Cash guy makes me so angry I could spit. There should have been a law against those people having children. He's just like his mother and father; they defy death. At least Millicent managed to get Doctors Green and Victor killed. But then she paid with her life. But a Cash? No way. We had to take out Caleb." He stared over at Ulysses and his assistant, Karl. "What can we do to root out the son? He and his merry band can't cause a stink in the news. We've got that covered. I don't see the weasels getting out of the state either. If they were in our compound, how did the hell did they get back out in the first place?"

"Guard error. Their photos are now on display as you enter and leave all exits. Unfortunately, our retina cameras didn't get close enough to ID their eyes."

"Very poor placement, Make arrangements to move them closer to the vehicle and pedestrian access gates." He sat in a chair next to the main station. "Think man. How can we snare them?"

Karl stepped forward. "I will be happy to take Fran and arrange for a snare game."

"Snare game?"

The short bald man nodded. You see, we go in search of these traitors to science and pretend we, like they, are countrymen who wish to escape from the evil intent of the Genetic Right. Then, we suggest they come with us to the compound instead of away toward the border. Nicky will do anything to follow Fran, so his regular logical mind will see no fallacy in this. I'll say I know how they can enter without getting caught, which of course, I'll bungle. You can capture them and all will be right with the world."

Devlin rubbed his chin. "Not very creative but almost stupid enough to work. Okay, Karl, take the clone, though I have no idea why. She's about as close to being a dumb blonde as one can be, even though she doesn't have that color hair."

"I'll go get ready and tell Fran." Karl left the room.

"I'm glad he left." Ulysses smiled and rubbed his

hands together. "Ready for a little surprise? One even Karl doesn't know about?"

Devlin turned, his interest piqued. "Go for it. Maybe it will improve my mood."

Ulysses motioned for him to follow. "There is another clone we have yet to wake up. One in whom you will be most interested." They went into a frigid room, where tubes lined the walls and cases displayed failed clone experiments. It looked like a morgue, only more frightening. Devlin straightened his shoulders. Forget about haunted houses. This was the real McCoy. They finally stopped at the back where a secure lock was affixed. Ulysses punched in a combination. "Behold the Primera."

Devlin walked in and over to the tube. The woman lay in repose, her skin like ash, but her short red hair vibrant.

"Well, I have to admit it." Devlin stared closer through the clear cryogenic transporopariethilene cylinder. "It looks exactly like her."

Ulysses nodded. "That's because it is. A perfect clone of the Primera, DNA samples taken from her before she died in the Emancipation Wars. They were kept in Antarctica until three months ago when the POPs were ordered to check the facilities for illegal activity. Thankfully, our plant down there got out with them before he was detected and flew them here quickly so as not to compromise the quality."

Devlin rubbed his hands together. "Wonderful, but don't wake her up just yet. Once Mil is back in full form, no one will budge without her permission. For a while I would like to maintain control."

Ulysses nodded. "As you wish."

***

Midday, they stopped in an overgrown area that afforded a small amount of relief from the direct sun beating down from overhead. Elle mopped off her forehead with a now filthy handkerchief. "I wish I had access to a tri-wave cycle wash machine. My clothes, government-issue, including the handkerchiefs, are recyclable, so unlike the disposable trash now available in the stores. But, out here, I wish I had clean stuff."

Wallace nodded. Another sign she was female. Men didn't care how dirty they got. Not in the outdoors, anyway.

"I hear a sound in the sage brush." Nicky sprinted to the fringe, and plunged through. Seconds later, he reappeared, pushing the weeds back out of the way. "A man and woman are coming toward us. They aren't close enough for me to get a fix on possible IDs."

Elle grabbed her long range optiglasses. "I'll check them out. Be back in a flash."

While Elle was gone, Wallace took his chance. "Just what did you hear last night, Nicky?"

He smiled. "Something that reminded me of a long time ago."

"Which was?" Wallace leaned in the sand on one propped-up arm.

"The sounds of love-making. There was no mistaking the groans."

"Sex, I hate to correct you. It was sex. Pure copulation and nothing else."

Nicky shook his head. "No, I know the difference. I have been there. It may have started as sex, but that didn't last very long. What you had last night was love-making. I'd stake my warranty on it."

Wallace didn't know how to answer the Andro. His gut churned at Nicky's words because his mind knew a part of what the Andro said rang true, and it scared the shit out of him. The last thing he needed to do was depend on another human being. It was too risky to the future he had mapped out for himself, a teacher, objective and set on his intellectual pursuits.

"They're from the lab, I think." Elle pushed through the brush. "The man has on a white jacket and the woman looks like the one Nicky described before his circuits fried."

Nicky stood, his body suddenly freezing in place.

"Don't you dare short-circuit again!" Wallace screamed. We can't carry you anywhere and we don't have a replacement cell."

Nicky blew out a breath and inhaled again. "I'll be all right. I've been practicing breathing exercises. That whole thing before would have been embarrassing to my 6052 brothers. Even if it is Fran, I will not blow a fuse. I swear."

Minutes later, a bald-headed man pushed back the same brush where Elle had entered. Then he halted, his eyes bulging, as he saw them. "Wow, didn't even hear you folks. Please excuse me for intruding. Just one moment." He disappeared for a second before returning. "I believe you may be the people we were searching for."

"You've got the stage." Elle crossed her arms. "Who are you and whoever is traveling with you and who were you trying to find?"

He moved forward. "My name is Karl Leipzeig. My assistant is with me and I asked that she stay where she is while I explain everything. I am a chemical and genetic scientist assigned to the Genetic Rights Laboratory. What GR employees at the lab are unaware of is the fact I am also a Cash Administration employee, part of the Special Forces and assigned by Raoul Martinez. My mission is to assist infiltrators who also work for the government. I was told a Cash would be here along with Raoul's own daughter."

"You are correct that Wallace Cash is with us and I am

Raoul's daughter, Elexia. I go by Elle." Elle advanced toward him. "But my father couldn't have known we were coming to the laboratory unless you spoke to him recently."

"No, not for at least a month."

"That's impossible." Wallace jumped up. "I didn't even know I'd be leaving the EC then."

"Kenada." Nicky smiled. "She knew. From the future, just like I said."

Wallace rolled his eyes. "I suppose now you're going to tell me she's been using the government's experimental bubble machine to time travel."

"I don't think she needs a machine."

"The Andro is correct." Karl placed his foot up on a rock. "I don't know about her being from the future, but Kenada is a well-known mystic and has been one hundred percent accurate on her predictions of what will occur. She's been advising the administration for some time."

"I don't get how she knows all that stuff." Wallace rubbed behind his ear. He stared over at Nicky. "And don't say anything about the future. I'll mull it over." Looking back at Karl, he smiled. "It's nice to have an ally with us. When are you going to ask your assistant to join you?"

"I thought I should explain first." Karl cleared his throat. "My assistant is a clone. She looks and acts like her former human self with one small exception. Because of the trauma that led to the original human's demise, the clone's brain appears to have altered so that the painful memories were erased. Some of her other memories, such as those that were deeply seeded, may have also suffered. I'm not sure how extensive these deficits are, but I am aware she has limited recall because I know a bit about her past."

He glanced toward Nicky. "For instance, I am aware my assistant, when she was still alive as the original human, was very fond of you, Andro. I believe your name is Nicky?"

Nicky nodded, his chin trembling.

"I should say tremendously so." Karl frowned. "I do not believe she remembers those emotions or you at all."

"It's Fran, isn't it?" Nicky's voice shook.

Karl nodded. "You must not pressure her. It may make her skittish. She has led a very sheltered life this time around, much as she did as the real Fran prior to escaping from the cryo lab in Nevada."

"I understand." Nicky stared at the ground and toed a clump of dirt. "What I remember about what happened the day she died will haunt me forever. No one has been able to remove that from my memory banks. It appears it is burned into them like a negative image. Thankfully, the human brain is more malleable."

"I don't know that what you say is so." Karl exhaled. "You would think that we would know more about the human brain after all these centuries, yet it is still a mystery in many ways." He shrugged. "Such is the enigma of human existence. If everyone is ready, I'll call her."

He walked back through the brush. "Fran, you can join us now." Karl reappeared and moved to one side as the weeds rustled and the woman looked out. Her short black hair was cropped close to her head. Bright blue eyes shone intelligently though dark lashes. Wallace thought she was remarkably beautiful, though not seeming as attractive to him as Elle.

"Fran!" Nicky ran forward and hugged her. "I can't believe you're here."

The woman stared at him, shock registering on her face as she pulled away from his embrace. "I beg your pardon, but I don't believe I've ever met you."

A ragged sob escaped Nicky's lips. "I…I am so sorry. You reminded me of someone I once knew and cared for deeply."

The new Fran nodded. "I understand. Please forgive me for being so inconsiderate of another's feelings. I'm afraid I often miss emotional cues. Karl tells me that's because of my past trauma, though I'm afraid I don't remember having any."

Nicky nodded as he walked away from the group, his

body visibly shaking.

"That could be a blessing." Wallace strode over to her and held put his hand. "I'm Wallace Cash. Elle Martinez and Nicky are helping me arrange for peace talks with the Genetic Right. So far, that seems to be an impossible task."

Fran smiled. "I would say it would never happen. I've overheard many discussions Karl and Ulysses have had with Mr. Hood. I would say the GR's leader has no intention of settling the administration. It appears he would prefer overthrowing it."

Karl nodded. "Fran's right. I've asked that she stay out of it, she really isn't capable of tackling the problem at this time, but I can tell you Devlin has escalated into extreme anger since you, Wallace, arrived in New Mexico."

"Isn't that just terrific?" Wallace chuckled. "How do you suggest we circumvent him?"

"I can't see any way you can except to eliminate him."

"Maybe we can reactivate the Freedom Fighters."

Wallace turned around and stared at Elle. "Don't you think they'd be a bit old by now? I don't see your dad out here fighting anymore."

She grinned. "He could and he'd beat your ass into the dirt. You're correct though, that most of his gang have hung up their weapons. However, that doesn't mean the Freedom Fighters have ceased to exist. The vigilante group is still here. It works out mostly on weekends and ensures the GR doesn't go so far as to cut the state off from the rest of the country."

"Mother said the GR has already closed the borders. It doesn't seem any freedom dudes are on duty right now. Or at least they aren't strong enough to do what they used to."

She raised an eyebrow. "I dare say they are. We haven't been listening to the news."

Nicky touched his temple. "Latest news from administration headquarters. The GR lost two men on the New Mexico border last night when snipers took them out at long distance range. Thereafter a banner was lifted on the hill above stating 'freedom reigns.'"

Wallace stared and turned around to the Andro. "Since when have you been connected to the administration network?"

"Always. I thought you knew that."

"But…"

"Nicky has the same government scrambled technology as your interphase." Elle shook her head. "I should have remembered that. We've had many assists available to us we didn't take advantage of as we should have."

"We need to move, folks." Karl pointed off in the distance. "Leave it to me when we get close to the lab GR encampment."

"How did you know we were going back there?"

"Kenada." Karl strode toward him. "But I'd have suggested you do so anyway. There is something in the back room of the cooling section that Ulysses has kept off-limits, even to me. I'm not sure if he has managed to finally crack the DNA code and mutate the human genome or of it's something else entirely. I just know that for a while now he's been fixating on creating mutations, mostly human with the ability to fly and perform other feats that are currently impossible for human beings."

"Then what are we waiting for? Let's go find out what's back there." Wallace started to walk forward, then stopped. "There's something nagging at the back of my mind."

Elle walked up next to him. "Like what?"

Wallace squinted. "I'm not sure. I keep thinking it's linked to something Kenada said, something she triggered, but since she always talks in riddles, I can't put my finger on it right now. It'll come to me. A nice brisk walk across the desert ought to do the trick."

Elle smirked. "All that does for me is produce hallucinations."

Chapter Six

"Well it *ain't* déjà vu all over again. Except now they have security patrolling like prison guards." Wallace watched in amazement from their hiding place. "The compound looks like ants are crawling all around it."

"They must know there are Freedom Fighters close by." Elle sat on the ground checking her neutron pistol and pulling more cartridges out of her knapsack and sticking them in her pockets. "Whoever invented these should get the Nobel Peace Prize."

Wallace smirked. "There's an oxymoron if I ever heard one. Peace through destruction. Great slogan."

Elle shrugged. "If it works, don't knock it."

"Hate to say it, but it's not working. Otherwise, Dad wouldn't be dead and neither would the squad."

"Good point, but these scientists don't count. They have the heads wrapped around experimentation and don't react like the general population. Besides, Devlin, their *leader*, is insane. Just calling him a leader makes me shudder. He makes Hitler look like a Sunday School teacher."

"She's right." Karl sighed. "They don't see him for what he is. It's almost like everyone there is in a trance. Including Fran, which is the most odd, since her former self wouldn't have stood for this injustice."

Wallace glanced over to where Fran was sitting on a rock. Nicky was right next to her, talking away like an animated comic character. "Look at that. Nicky's talking twice his normal speed. He wants things to be the way it used to be. It's sad."

"Happily-ever-after only happens in fairy tales."

Wallace frowned as he looked back at Elle. "Your parents were happy, weren't they? I know mine were."

"They're not now. Face it Wallace, there's happily-ever-after and after happily ever, which is never happy."

Wallace rubbed the back of his neck. "Now *you're* talking in riddles. Kenada is rubbing off on you."

"Not Kenada, just reality."

Nicky strode back to them and stared down. "Hey folks, I know what's wrong with Fran. She's been chipped."

Wallace jerked to attention. "Impossible. No human's been chipped in more than fifty years."

"Not impossible and it's not a privacy chip. This is an obedience one like the Primera used to implant in the Antarctica prisoners of war. I daresay that is the reason for her gap in memory."

"That's because you want it to be so." Wallace rested his hand on Nicky's shoulder.

Nicky nodded. "I'd love for it to be so, but I also know the signs of obedience chipping. Dull affect, faraway eyes, animated speech, little interaction with others. They're all classic indicators."

Karl's head jerked up, his eyes widening. "He's right." Karl strode over. "Ulysses said Fran had disobeyed commands when she first came to the compound. I never caught on that they'd done anything to her because she was placed in the facility by the government to observe experimentation. It was a given she'd ruffle some feathers. I was told to make contact with her. At first Ulysses said she had always been like that, but then mentioned he'd been told that prior to her arrival she'd had surgery because of nightmares and painful memories. He claimed he didn't know what those were."

Nicky nodded. "He was covering in case you found the incision site. Front lobe just behind the hairline. It's not placed in the nape of the neck like the old tracking chips. I checked. Fran has the incision scar."

Wallace balled his fists at his sides. She'd been treated

like an old war criminal that'd had a lobotomy. These people would stop at no atrocity to have their way. He turned to Elle. "Do you know how to remove that kind of chip?"

She shook her head. "I'm not a surgeon and I wasn't trained the way the old guerillas were. Dad knew how. I've heard him talk about it, and I dare say someone in his old group knows how to as well."

"Have any idea where we can find the Freedom Fighters?"

A man in all camo stepped out of the brush. "You rang?"

Elle stood with her gun in her hand. "How long have you been there?"

"As long as you've been here. I've been trailing after you the last couple of miles. Bruno Ramos at your service." He clicked his heels together and bowed his head.

"Nice to meet you Bruno, if that's who you really are." Elle's eyes narrowed on the soldier. "Prove you're really a Freedom Fighter. You should know how to do it."

"Raoul Martinez says drop to the ground, soldier, and do fifty." He grinned, showing bright white teeth against his olive skin.

"That's the code?" Wallace chuckled. "Who knew your dad had a sense of humor?"

"No surprise. He's normally happy."

"But not funny." He shook his head. "I should have known it would be screwy."

"I'm ignoring that Grunt. Bruno, you pass. I'm Elle Martinez, Raoul's daughter, and this is Wallace Cash. I doubt I have to explain the Cash part. The Andro is Nicky. The rest are…"

"No need. I heard all about them while I watched you."

Elle smiled. "You're very good at tailing." She put her gun away. "Where are the rest of the troops?"

"In the mountains, the Anasazi caves. However, the location moves."

She nodded. "It has to. The FF have been making those their home base for decades. Let's cut to the chase. Do you known how to remove an obedience chip?"

He pulled out a long slender knife from his jacket. "Does a surgeon have a scalpel?"

Wallace laughed nervously. "I suggest we get Fran to your headquarters and we can take care of going into the compound afterwards. That also gives us more backup, a better plan and one more person who has all her faculties in order."

Bruno smiled. "Follow me. There's a small band of us staying about a half mile away. It's not the caves, but there we can take care of Fran faster and then get back to the compound."

"There isn't much time to waste." A shadow fell over Karl's face. "If we wait too long, Devlin will suspect I've double-tricked them and you'll never get into their science building again."

"We'll have to be fast." The muscles in Wallace's shoulders tensed.. "Let's get hopping, Bruno. Where do we go?"

***

Ulysses stood over the clear coffin-shaped container that held the Primera's clone. He ached to wake her. She was a leader. She should be theirs now as she once has been, not the Cash woman who had assumed charge after the Emancipated States. His work would progress much faster with Mil in command. The mutations would be living breathing creatures, not cultures in Petri dishes. There was no doubt about it. The current administration was bent on the destruction of both cloning and genetic mutation—except as permitted for improvement of food products. Nothing more. He wouldn't let that happen.

He had thought Devlin Hood would be their answer. It now seemed that the man was more interested in his own power than the good of science. Because of that Ulysses had decided to defy orders. Millicent Davis would be awake before Hood could stop the process. Then they'd be on the right track and would have a caveat—the Cash son, for by then he would have arrived. Ulysses rubbed his hands together from the anticipation of using some of Cash's DNA for the mutations before the man was destroyed. What sweet justice!

Ulysses smiled as he started the timer. In twenty hours, the Primera could once again continue her mission and so could he.

***

Nicky collapsed on a rock. "I don't want to ever go through that again."

"Your skin looks pasty." Wallace reached out a trounced the Andro's forehead. "Since when do you sweat? Your head is cold and clammy."

"I have begun to for a while." He stared at the ground. "My cooling system must be malfunctioning."

"Or your heart is beginning to assume control of your functions." Elle smiled. "I'm beginning to figure this out. Nicky, I think you're different from your fellow 6052s. I think you are an experimental model who was made in the likeness of its creator. I'd be willing to bet you have a bloodstream as well as a coolant track."

"That doesn't make any sense." Wallace stood. "To have an Andro with parts that can wear out is ludicrous. Why would anyone do it?"

"I don't know." Elle threw her arms in the air. "I don't know much these days. My guess is the man who did it was leaving his mark behind."

272

Nicky laughed. "Wallace is afraid I'm more virile than he is. He should be nervous. I can go all night long."

Elle smiled. "Sorry, Nicky. I don't think he has anything to worry about."

Bruno walked back to where they were and collapsed in the dirt. "That was harder than they told me it would be."

"What do you mean?" Wallace stared at the man. It was hard for a person of Hispanic descent to appear white, but Bruno had done it. "Haven't you performed that surgery before?"

Bruno stared up at Wallace. "Are you crazy man? Do you think I do that for pleasure? Now, how many people do you think are walking around with obedience chips?"

"He did all right, Wallace." Nicky stared at him. "I watched his every move, and I know what's supposed to happen. I just couldn't do it. He could, and did it well."

"That makes a lot of good sense. Nicky. Bruno is to be congratulated." Elle laid her hand on his shoulder. "That must have been difficult for you and for Bruno."

"It was." Bruno and Nicky said it at the same time and exchanged nodding glances.

Nicky gazed off in the distance. "Karl's already with Fran, but I'm going to go back and stay at her side until she wakes up. It will make me happy if she remembers me, if only a little."

"I hope it happens, and I guess it's time for all of us to sleep." Elle pulled her blanket roll off the knapsack.

"You can sleep in the tent over there." Bruno pointed at a makeshift one made with a camo tarp, strung across bushes and staked with twigs and twine. "It's large enough for two." His gaze turned to Wallace. "I just thought more than one of you might want cover."

"Thanks, Bruno." Wallace chuckled. "You're okay."

Then they were alone. Wallace glanced over at Elle. "You've been distant today. Rethinking what we did last night?"

She didn't look at him. "Maybe. I'm thinking about a lot of things. What if we can't bring peace, Wallace? What if Kenada is wrong? Or what if we can but it isn't in time for us to keep the experimentation from reaching out and consuming the future? This whole thing is scary and it seems impossible two people could solve the problem in such a short time frame."

He nodded as he strode to her and turned her around to face him, his hands clasping her waist on each side. "Maybe you're scared of even more. Tonight is the first time you've seemed vulnerable. Even with our wild love-making last night, you never seemed to budge from the warrior, ready to conquer. But tonight it's different. Tonight, you seem like you aren't as sure and are ready for someone else to take charge."

She reached out and circled his waist with her arms. "Maybe I am. Are you ready to lead Wallace Cash?"

He grinned. "I'm ready to love, really love. And now I think I also know how to lead. Because I finally know the secret to success. Leading isn't about being tough and in control. Leading isn't being right all the time or always knowing the answer, but letting all those who follow have input. A true leader must make decisions, but true leadership come from the heart, not the mind."

She laughed, but tears ran down her face. "I can't believe you said that."

He looked at her, confused, as he brushed the tears from her eyes. "Why?"

She sniffed. "Because Dad has told me the same thing since I was a child."

He drew her closer. "I bet your dad hasn't ever done this." Wallace bent to take her mouth, intent on making love to her, not rushing her, as his tongue teased her mouth opened and entered it. She met him with her own as she sucked back. He felt his cock spring to life, but he wasn't about to rush this. What they were doing was about more than sex. Nicky had been right. This was what making love was all about, and she fit him better than any woman ever could. He could feel it in her response and the way they flowed together like the same stream.

As he deepened his kiss, he heard a coyote in the

distance howling at the moon. Maybe there was some truth to Kenada's tale.

Chapter Seven

Wallace woke to the sound of footsteps outside the tent. He crawled over Elle's still sleeping body and peaked outside. Nicky stood there, his mouth a grim line. Sliding further to the edge of the enclosure, Wallace inched out. Elle stirred once but rolled over as he made his way out of the tent.

Motioning for Nicky to move back, he got to his feet and pointed to the rocks they'd sat on the night before. Once they were seated, he placed his hand on Nicky's shoulder. "What's troubling you, my friend?"

"Fran is awake. She still doesn't remember who I am."

"Oh." Wallace reached out and hugged the Andro to him, then pulled back. "I know it isn't customary for a man to hug another one, but you looked like you could use it."

Nicky nodded as he stared at the ground. "Thank you

for calling me a man. That in itself is a compliment."

"You are more of a man than most I've known."

Nicky blew out a long breath. "Right now it would be easier to be just an Andro. As for Fran, she is much more talkative than she was and I can see the old fighting spirit *my Fran* had returning just in the couple of hours she's been awake."

"You see? The removal of the chip did some good. Who knows? Her memory may come back to her in time."

"Or she never will remember." His mouth trembled. "It's like I just lost her all over again."

"Concentrate on the mission, Nicky. For now it will make you feel better. Wishing something is true won't make it that way. That's the reason we have to learn patience. Only time will tell the story."

"You're right." Nicky stared out along the path leading down towards the compound. "I believe I'll go sneak around their headquarters and see if I can learn anything. "I'll be back later today and let everyone know what I discover. We are still planning on setting out tomorrow morning, aren't we?"

"That's our plan unless we discover we must move faster."

With a final nod, Nicky turned and walked down the path and out of sight.

"You've changed a lot, Wallace."

He turned and saw Elle striding toward him.

"When you came here you had little compassion. Then you never would have hugged Nicky, nor would you have spoken the words you just said."

"You're right. I feel different." Wallace leaned to one side on the rock. "I think it's because I witnessed the uselessness of the deaths of all those soldiers and then saw Nicky's sorrow over Fran. I realized how fragile life can be, even if cloning is possible. What matters is what's happening now, and it's human to comfort each other. Even if the human is half-mechanical." He tried to grin.

"You did the right thing. Come on and let's get some grub."

As they made their way to the center of the camp, five men sat cross-legged, four fighters and Karl, chowing down on nutrition bars. "Come join us compadres." Bruno gestured to them. "We have enough to share. Too bad we cannot afford to start a fire."

"I wouldn't mind one of those five-legged jackrabbits about now." Wallace walked forward and sat next to Bruno. "However, I will gladly accept one of those bars."

"No need." Kenada slipped through the wild grass and placed a large sack of food next to the men. "I brought supplies."

Wallace leaned his head to one side. "You said your staying behind was as it should be."

279

"It was. Then. Now it is deemed right to be here." Kenada eased to the ground, her feet crossed.

Bruno stared at her, his mouth wide open. "I want to know how you got past all my guards."

Opening the sack, Kenada poured the food containers onto the sandy soil. "I did not pass them."

Bruno threw his arms open. "But you had to pass them. They're positioned all around this area."

"Don't waste your breath." Wallace touched Bruno's arm. "Believe me, you aren't going to get a better answer."

Smiling, Kenada leaned forward. "The wind blows the answers through time and whispers in my ears. I go where it beckons and speak what I'm told."

"See?" Wallace chuckled.

"I think I'll depend on science instead of what the wind tells me." Karl took another bite from his bar.

"As a Freedom Fighter you do not question fate." Bruno's eyes never left Kenada. "If what you say is true, tell me woman, what did the wind tell you?"

She bowed her head. "Trouble brews in the false land of creation. The creators split and hope to conquer. Evil rises from sleep and walks among the living. The dark shadow of the son of death waits to pounce among the unsuspecting."

"How about telling us who and where these people are?"

"I cannot. I speak only what I am told." Kenada bowed her head.

"The false land of creation must be the lab in the compound." Elle reached for a can of food. "The dark shadow of the son of death sounds a lot like Devlin Hood to me."

"How about the creators splitting and the evil rising from sleep?" Wallace leaned his elbows back behind him.

Elle shrugged. "I don't know. Maybe it all has to do with whatever creation they're working on? They hope to multiply it?"

Kenada sat bolt upright, her eyes wide with fear. "You must go now. Linger and perish."

Bruno cursed under his breath. "Did the wind just whisper that?"

"I simply know. No time to wait."

Wallace scrambled to his feet. "Last time she said that, the men and our headquarters were obliterated." He stared at Bruno. "I suggest you tell everyone to pack up and get ready because we better get jetting along. Maybe we can catch up to Nicky."

***

"Why did you wait to wake me?" Millicent sat on the table and stared at Ulysses.

"Mr. Hood told me to."

She glared at him. "Hood is dead. He died years

before those assholes fried me."

"It is his son."

Millicent stood. "Hmm, now that you mention it I do vaguely remember he had one. The widow was such a wimp. I should have known Hood's son would be ready to take charge. The apple doesn't fall far from the tree. Unfortunately I haven't indoctrinated this one. Pity. He'll have to go." She stared down at her nails and frowned. She doubted they had anyone here to give her a manicure. She did so hate to be lacking in appearance when going to war. "You say Caleb Cash's son is here trying to stop experimentation?"

Ulysses nodded. "Yes, Madam Primera. Karl has gone to retrieve him."

Her face burned at the thought of another progeny. "It appears the Cash men all will be like William. One fuck and they pop out a kid. Too bad William didn't have his with the right woman. So be it. Is this Wallace the only son Caleb had?"

"That is correct."

She grinned. "Then let's get rid of him before he fathers a son. What are you waiting for? Show me out of this deepfreeze and let's get on with locating him. No doubt there will be only a short window of time until that bitch, Winnifred, discovers her worst enemy is back."

***

282

"I'm fine, really." Fran touched the bandage on her head. "My head only hurts a little. But I am no longer in a fog. Let's go annihilate the bastards."

"Sounds like she's back to normal to me." Elle shook her hand. "Welcome Fran. Dad will be glad to see you after this is over."

"Win too, I hope." Fran stared at the ground. "Why don't I remember Nicky? He seemed so hurt I didn't."

"Don't worry." Wallace tried to smile. "It'll come to you, I'm sure."

As the men all marched forward, Fran and Elle following, Wallace turned to Kenada. She still sat on the ground. "You're coming this time, aren't you?"

She shook her head. "It is as it should be."

"Well of all the…"

She placed her finger to her lips. "Listen and do not argue. I waited until everyone left. The ally is not a friend. It is he who guards against you."

Wallace placed both hands on his hips. "What the hell are you trying to tell me?"

"All will become clear. You must go."

Grumbling, he threw up his hands and stomped off. "Damned psychic nut. Gives you riddles for answers and answers that don't make sense. Since when have I started believing in readings? This is crazy, I…" Wallace halted in his tracks and grinned. Could it be he was beginning to figure out what Kenada was saying? He ran to catch up with Elle. "Hey, do you remember when I told you that it was hard to forget what the Primera did to us?"

"Of course."

"When we were in the bunker, Kenada answered, 'It's not over yet.'"

"So?"

"The Primera. They're bound to have cloned her. That's what Ulysses is hiding."

"Maybe."

"No, it is." Wallace took a deep breath. "One riddle solved. Now I have two more."

"What were they?"

He shook his head. "That's okay. I think I'm the one who has to figure them out."

An hour later, they closed in on the compound. "Looks like when we left it." Wallace squinted as he watched the guards patrolling. "I wonder where Nicky is."

"Don't worry about him." Elle stared through her binoculars. "He made it through the Emancipation Wars. I'd say he knows how to maneuver."

"Maybe, but he almost didn't come out of the wars in one piece."

Fran frowned. "What happened to him?"

Wallace froze. "Uh. I supposed you'll have to ask him that yourself."

Karl crawled up next to them. "I'm going to lead the men around back. You and Elle need to come in from the left of the compound. There is one blind spot not covered by guards or cameras."

"How can that be?" Wallace leaned on one arm and stared at the man. "If you know about it, surely security has to have figured that out."

Karl raised his eyebrows. "I don't know. All I can say is that's the way we get illegal alcohol into the lab."

Wallace nodded. He knew alcohol was a hot commodity in some states. The GR had gotten it banned in New Mexico. So why did he question Karl's words? Once again, Kenada's words rang in his ears. *The ally is not a friend.* "Bruno?"

Bruno scrambled over on his elbows and knees. "Yes, compadre?"

"Take Karl into custody."

Karl laughed. "That's a joke, right?"

As Wallace turned toward him, Karl sprang to his feet, sprinting toward open ground. Elle pulled her neutron pistol and fired. Karl dropped to the ground. "Nothing like short range radiation." She grinned. "I'm glad technology figured out how to harness it so it doesn't spread."

"We can only hope the guards don't detect him right away." Bruno stood and waved at the men. "We need to skirt right. Considering what Karl wanted us to do, I believe that is our best bet to deter detection."

"If I'm right, one of those guards is Raoul's other plant." Wallace stared at Elle. "Great shooting. I don't think my hand would've been that steady."

"Practice." She put up the gun. "Dad had me on a firing range when I was four."

"Why does that not surprise me?" Wallace pulled out his interphase.

"What are you doing?" Elle leaned over.

"I'm telling Mother to bomb the hell out of this compound in one hour. The time for negotiations is over. Between then and now, we need to locate Nicky."

His mother's face blinked on. "I was just getting ready to call you."

"Why?"

"Millicent Davis' clone is back in charge. She's inside the GR headquarters."

Wallace nodded. "I figured that out. We need to bomb it. One hour. I just need to find Nicky first."

"I hate to tell you this. They have Nicky."

He stared blankly at the screen. "They?"

"Millicent Davis is threatening to destroy him and your squad if I don't denounce my seat."

"Mother, she'll do that anyway."

"I am aware of that." A tear rolled down her cheek. "Wallace, be careful."

He nodded. "I will, Mom." He turned off the interphase. "Let's move out."

***

Devlin stopped on a dime as he stared into Millicent's eyes. "Primera." He kneeled before her. "I had no idea they had succeeded in cloning you. I was the one who told them to continue with their efforts."

She shook her head. "Stop the bullshit. Ulysses told me the truth and I don't think he was the one who was lying."

"You know how faithful my father was to you." Devlin stood. "He died for your cause. Do you honestly think I'd deceive you?"

Millicent rolled her eyes. "I think you'd deceive your own mother if you could garner more power. Too bad you have to be terminated. You remind me of me."

"But…"

She pulled out an old fashioned pistol and shot him between the eyes. "Lead still works." She turned to a security guard. "Get rid of this mess. I hate trash. Let me know as soon as you have Cash in custody. I'll go tell Ulysses Devlin's taken care of."

"He's not there Madam Primera."

She turned on her heel and stared at the guard. "What do you mean he's not there?"

"He left the building an hour ago with a bunch of

equipment. Said something about protecting all the experimentation."

"Honestly." Millicent put the gun down. "No one has any faith in me, anymore." Millicent patted the side of her hair. "Even though I'm back to my early-twenties. I'm prime and loaded for bear. Winnifred Davis isn't a spring chicken anymore, and besides, she doesn't have enough nerve to bomb this building. Not with her precious Android here."

She glanced over at Nicky, bound and gagged in the corner. "Winnifred isn't aware I know about your real heart, Andro. I can kill you just like I can any man. Bad manufacturing process. Works for me, though. And I do love a show. When Wallace Cash gets here, it's show time!"

***

As they skirted the right side of the encampment, Wallace saw a guard standing there, his gun on the ground. "What the…"

The man pulled out a Cash campaign flag and waved it in the air.

Elle chuckled. "Looks like we found our real ally."

"Guess so. The way must be clear. He slipped down alongside the guard. "Wallace Cash."

"Kurt Satterwhite, your contact, and I know who you are, Elexia. Just talked to Raoul." He nodded to the men behind Wallace. "Tell them to go around back. The guards are already dead."

"Fast work."

"I'm trained to do it."

"I'm going with you and Elle." Fran stepped up to where he stood.

"You're still weak. You'll be better off surrounded by Bruno and his squad."

She shook her head. "Nicky is in there. I know he means something to me. I just don't know what. I'm going with you."

Elle glanced up at Wallace. "I'm not going to argue with her."

Wallace shook his head. "Women. Okay, Kurt, lead on."

Minutes later they stood outside the door to main station of operations. "Are you sure they're in there?"

Kurt nodded. "I had a plant inside to watch the door. Ulysses went out a long time ago with two large hard backed cases. He left the grounds, flew off in a water jet. Devlin arrived, went in and my plant heard a gun go off. The guard dragged out a body and put it in the incinerator. No one else came out."

"Where is this plant now?"

"Close enough." Kurt grinned.

Fran grabbed Wallace's hand. "Do you think the body

was Nicky's?"

"Doubtful," Elle said, interrupting. "Millicent Davis would want to make his death a warning to others. She needs an audience."

Wallace glanced at the guard. "Let's go say hello. Do the honors, Kurt."

The man stepped forward and slowly opened the door letting it swing back. Wallace looked inside, panic seizing him as he saw Millicent Davis, just like her pictures, standing in the back of the room with a bound and gagged Nicky, a pistol against his chest.

Millicent glared at him, her eyes narrowing to slits. "Honest to God, does every Cash man have to look like William?"

Wallace puffed out his chest. "I'm proud to look like Gramps and my dad."

She smirked. "Get over it. If you don't drop your weapons and turn yourself in, your little Andro, human hybrid is going to die in front of your eyes."

"Nicky!" Fran screamed at the top of her lungs, launching herself in front of Wallace, aiming her neutron pistol and shooting Millicent dead center in the chest.

The pistol fell from the Primera's hand as she fell backward onto the floor.

Fran ran forward, dropping her own gun as she made her way to Nicky. She bent to take the gag off his mouth.

Wallace stared at Elle. "Wow. That has to be the shortest of Millicent's lives."

She laughed. "There's nothing like the element of surprise."

As the gag came off Nicky's mouth. Fran bent and gave him a kiss.

"I think she remembers who he is."

Elle smiled up at Wallace. "Do you think?"

He glanced back at the guard. "Is the whole camp contained?"

"Absolutely. We don't have many prisoners. There are probably some scientists still hiding out in the mountains. We'll start searching for Ulysses."

"Do that pronto. But first, help Fran untie her man" Wallace put his arm around Elle's shoulders. "Care to go for a walk?"

She looked into his eyes, a puzzled expression on her face. "Okay, mind if you tell me why?"

"I don't know, maybe I want to ask you something."

She smiled. "Such as?"

"Will you stop calling me Grunt?"

"Oh." She looked down. "I thought it might be something else."

He tilted her head up and kissed her mouth. "I haven't gotten to the proposal," he whispered inches from her mouth.

"What kind?"

He grinned. "Is it okay if our kid looks like Gramps?"

We hope you enjoyed
The Rise and Fall of Millicent
Other Fantasy Books by this author
writing as Daryn Cross:

Walk Right In, L&L Dreamspell
Walk Right Back, L&L Dreamspell
Honey Blood and the Collector, Turquoise Morning
Press
Witchy Woman of the Downs, Turquoise Morning
Press
It's Magic, Crescent Moon Press
This Magic Moment, Turquoise Morning Press

Books by the author, writing as Bobbye Terry

The Lipstick Girls –
Pucker Up – Print Compilation, coming in 2013

Briny Bay Mysteries-A cozy mystery novella series
Turquoise Morning Press

Buried in Briny Bay
The Marriage Murders
The Shadow Knows
A Murder in Every Port
Climax, Virginia Mystery Series

Coming to Climax
Nick of Time

ABOUT THE AUTHOR

Bobbye Terry is an award-winning author in both fiction and nonfiction and has also won awards for her poetry. She penned five published novels and numerous short-stories in collections with co-writer Linda Campbell under the pseudonym, Terry Campbell and since then has written. a couple of dozen books solo as Bobbye Terry and Daryn Cross. Her next fictional book will be *Nothing Ever Happens in Briny Bay*, released by Turquoise Morning Press in the summer of 2013. Her next inspirational book, *Joy Glows,* will also be released in the summer of 2013.

EXCERPT FROM

HONEY BLOOD AND THE COLLECTOR

Turquoise Morning Press

©2012

CHAPTER ONE

Slaying vampires was Honey Draper's fulltime job.

Especially since she lived in Transylvania.

In a castle.

And owned a pet dragon.

Okay, so she lived in Transylvania County, North Carolina, her castle was an estate on a mountain overlooking Lake Toxaway, and both vampires and her pet dragon didn't exist as far as modern-day humans were concerned. But what did humans know? Vampires found her regularly, and Cinder was not a figment of her imagination. Honey could prove it right now by the soot marks on her face.

She wiped the smudges off with a cotton

ball and baby oil. "Cinder, really. Cover your mouth when you sneeze." Honey picked some mineral make-up and a brush and began to repair the bare spot.

Her baby giggled, thumping a fifty-pound tail.

Shaking her head, Honey looked at Cinder in the mirror. "I don't know what I'm going to do with you when you're twice your size." She sighed. "Thankfully, you won't grow that much for another hundred years."

Honey thought about those first days only fifty years ago when she'd brought Cinder home as a newly weaned hatchling. Back then her claws were nonexistent and her scales bent like rubber. But the little one had come equipped with one scorching case of dragon breath.

Unable to control her characteristic fire balls at such an early age, the dragonette's uncontrolled bursts of flame singed the draperies and the carpet, and, on one occasion, almost set the great room ablaze. Thank God for Uncle Mortie's intuitive powers.

"At least now, your flames are under control. Almost." Honey dropped the brush and make-up in her cosmetic tray and twirled for Cinder. "How do I look?"

The dragon grinned by flicking her forked tongue between upwardly drawn jowls and thumped her tail three times, a sign she approved.

Honey ran her hand over Cinder's recently manicured scales. "Thanks, sweetie. You do so know how to give a girl a compliment. Have to look good for the country club art auction, you know. The auction'll bring in a lot of money for the new heart wing at the hospital. Heaven knows we need more money to ensure people have the care they need. Especially with the vampire population abounding around here."

She kissed the baby on her snout and exited the bathroom, making her way down the winding staircase.

Descending past the gigantic crystal

chandelier hanging in the center of the vaulted ceiling, she entered the huge great room below. A fire crackled in the massive stone fireplace on the far wall in front of her, and the smell of roasted turkey wafted past her nose.

"Damn it to thunder, I'd rather stay here," Honey grumbled, knowing it wasn't an option. Uncle Mortimer had insisted her role in tonight's affair was *non-negotiable*. Funny word for him to use, but he *was* the leader of their line. What he said, one did, even if you were one-hundred-ninety-six, the human equivalent of twenty-eight years old.

"I'm going now, Uncle Mortie," she called out to him.

He poked his head around the doorframe to the kitchen. "All right darling. Be careful, and keep your eyes peeled for a tall blond-haired man in a tux with a red rose in the lapel."

She narrowed her eyes. "Is he a vampire?"

He shook his head. "No, but I think

you'll want to meet him."

She cocked her head sideways. "Whatever for?"

He placed his forefinger on his temple and winked.

She exhaled sharply and shook her head at her uncle's way of telling her it was for him to know and her to find out. "Whatever. I'll be back by ten. Save me some turkey."

He laughed. "Always. And darling, also watch out for vampirinas. I sense they're close by. Besides, I caught a whiff of rotting B.O."

"Yeah, yeah." She waved, then grabbed her beaded evening purse from the side table. Closing the front door behind her, she fished in it and pulled out her laser stake. "I may as well have given my sixth toe for this," she sighed, as she placed it back in the bag. To think the modern laser version of the old hawthorn stake took up less than one tenth of the space of the old one and eliminated the need for a hammer. "Its best feature," she murmured to herself, "is the thousand-year warranty." She grinned. It could strike a vamp dead at the first beam.

She clicked her purse shut and bounded down the steps in her ballet flats. *You can't be too careful when you're an Ieie.*

Moments later, she entered the stately one floor clubhouse and made her way to the main dining room. It was closed this evening to normal dining and had been decorated in red and pink to celebrate its theme of "Keep Hearts Pumping." Red wine fountains gushed at the center display, and a string quartet played from the far end, near the long span of doors leading to the outside porch overlooking the golf course.

"Honey B." A small gray-haired lady with a pug nose and wild eyebrows excitedly inched her way across the floor in a too-tight full-length silver evening dress. "Thank the dear Lord you're here. I thought I might have to give the opening address, and considering how this dress shrank when I had it dry-cleaned, I didn't have a prayer of a chance of getting through a speech without swooning."

Honey grinned at her. "Not to worry, Mrs. Kirby. I'm here with five minutes to spare."

"Make yourself comfortable at the presentation table, and I'll get us started."

Honey sat down in the chair at the end of the long, linen-covered table. As Mrs. Kirby rang the small dinner bell shrilly, a loud boom resounded through the hall. All the candles flickered as a whoosh of air passed through, nearly extinguishing them. A rumble vibrated under their feet. Then the noises ended as quickly as they'd come and the odor of ozone filled the air.

"Oh my," the old woman said, her eyes wide with terror. "Whatever caused that sound?"

Honey stood and walked swiftly to the mic. "Ladies and gentlemen, don't be alarmed and keep your seats. We must have had a small tremor, that's all."

"Third time this week we had one," Mr. Kirby mumbled to his wife.

Honey saw a man enter the room, adjusting his cuffs and straightening his bow tie. Tall, toned, and tanned. That summed him up completely. A stray strand of blond hair fell down on his high forehead, and there was no mistaking the red rose he wore on his lapel. She eyed him slowly with interest.

Without question, he'd just annihilated a vampire.

****

"Why are you here?"

He turned as the "lady in red" approached him from behind and clicked his heels together. "Crawford Miklos at your service. I'm here primarily to write a check for a hundred thousand to charity. But, call me old fashioned, I prefer introductions before getting down to talking shop."

He watched as she blushed in embarrassment. "Of course. Honey Draper. Most people call me Honey B."

"Ah. As I expected," he said. *But they didn't tell me about those hypnotizing green eyes.* Or the honey red hair. Or, most intriguing of all, the defiant way she stood, daring him to cross her.

"I see," she said. "Someone *did* send you here to meet me. Uncle Mortie just said to watch out for a tall man with a red rose in his lapel."

"Watch out for or seek out?" he asked with a chuckle. "Big difference."

She raised an eyebrow. "I believe he meant I find you, but Uncle Mortie is rarely specific and never divulges everything he sees. He's a psychic."

"Really?" Crawford said, leaning back against the wall and crossing his legs nonchalantly. "I thought he was an elvan leader with Ieie blood."

"You know about Ieie blood?" Her eyes flickered like bright green flames.

"That it's the rarest blood type in the entire world? Unknown to the human race? Characterized as Type ABC? And possessed by less than three dozen elves in existence? Yes. I also know it drives vampires wild." He licked his finger and then turned on what women said was his *lady killer grin*.

"Okay, cut the crap," she whispered. "We both know you killed a vampire just outside this building less than an hour-and-a-half ago. What the hell is going on?"

She said it with the same fire in her eyes. He grinned. He'd always liked them feisty and high spirited. "Ah, here we are again, already talking shop." He stood up straight and shrugged. "If we must."

He stared down intently at her. "I was destined to meet you. The rest will become clear in its own good time. As for the vampire, let's just call him an appetite enhancer, you know, something to stir up the blood and get the juices flowing?" He eyed her with his best predatory look. "Other activities work even better."

He grabbed her, pulling her tightly against his body, and kissed her like it was the first and the last time. She responded as though she understood. Her body shook, growing wet with fresh perspiration as she bent into his embrace.

In the far background, he heard the gasps of onlookers. Spurred by the noise, like a red flag to a bull, he deepened his embrace, sliding his tongue between her teeth and playing with her own. She tasted like ripe black currants, a hint of vanilla and a heaping scoop of raw, reckless sex.

Then, knowing this could continue far into the night if he allowed it, but also aware he was best served to end it, he stopped and released her. His breath was labored, and he struggled to conceal his reaction from her.

Crawford watched as Honey stumbled back a step and caught her balance, while all the while self-consciously touching her swollen lips. Realizing his overpowering lust was breaking its bounds, a monster stampeding to have its way, he turned on his heel and proceeded to walk out.

"Wait."

He looked back over his shoulder. "Yes?"

Her jaw had dropped and her face was beet red. "Aren't you going to give me any more *information*?"

"Small doses, *dragostea mea*." And then in a low voice only she could hear, he added, "Don't bother to try and follow me. *I* can disappear too."

EXCERPT FROM

THIS MAGIC MOMENT

By Daryn Cross

Turquoise Morning Press

©2012

CHAPTER ONE

"It's dead and the only way you can save it is resurrection."

"For crying out loud, Zack! It's Christmas Eve!"

"So what? We've got one month until the Super Bowl and our commercial's flat."

Zack Graham strode toward the elevators. Staring at Mike Kramer, he wondered what was wrong with his cousin and VP of sales. The guy was acting like a green exec, not a man who'd weathered the worst on their way up the ladder.

Mike pulled to a stop beside him in front of the closed doors and glared at him. "It's fixable."

"Fixable?"

Mike stood there, his face twitching out of control. If Zack didn't know better he'd have sworn the guy had a disorder. Zack shook his head in concern. His cousin was coming unglued. Stress was something few people could handle like he could. The kid... Zack winced, silently correcting himself. The *twenty-five-year-old man* should be able to handle things better than this. He let out a deep breath as Mike finally nodded.

"Yeah, fixable."

Zack whistled. "Get with the program. Right now it doesn't have a pulse. And if we don't figure out how to resuscitate it, more than a million's flushed down the toilet."

"What do you want me to do?" Mike threw his arms out wide in that over-exaggerated gesture he made.

"Get downstairs to marketing, now, and kick some ass."

The doors of the elevators opened. At the sight of the full elevator, Zack started to count.

At three, he waved it on.

"Why not let the marketing department work on it by itself?"

Cringing at Mike's desperate tone, Zack turned and fixed on him with a laser-sharp gaze. "You can't trust anything to get done unless you stay on top of it, especially in this season of good cheer and idle carelessness."

Mike grabbed Zack's shoulder. "Look, George is our Director of Marketing and a twenty-year veteran. He can handle it, at least until New Year's."

"Never let down, Mike." Zack rubbed his forehead. Had he not taught his friend and executive anything? "Never let down, or the competition will pass you. Wipe you out. Every snack cake company's out there waiting for Scrumbles to slip."

Taking a deep breath, he glanced back at Mike. "Just a hint of weakness and the vultures attack. They'll gobble us up faster than you can eat one of our double chocolate chip delights. I've saved this corporation once. We've successfully diversified out of tobacco, and I'm not gonna let some conglomerate get their hooks into us. This is an American employee-held enterprise. And it's going to stay that way."

"Right."

Zack watched the doors of the elevator open again. Full. He waved it on.

"How many elevators are we going to wait on, cuz?"

He ground his teeth at the humor in Mike's voice. "Oh hell, let's take the stairs. It's good exercise." Zack strode towards the nearest exit door.

"We're on the fifteenth floor."

Zack bounded down the stairs. To hell if he'd waste precious time. This place would be emptying out like rats deserting a sinking ship for a holiday which was only meant for children.

"Cuz," Mike puffed, "don't you have to be somewhere for Christmas? I mean...don't you have a girlfriend, someone you want to spend some time with?"

Stopping and pivoting on the stairs, he glared at Mike. "I don't have time for a girlfriend."

"Neither do I," Mike muttered.

He stared at him, puzzled. "I thought you had one."

"I do. Gretta? I'm supposed to be spending tonight and the next couple of days in New York with her, remember? I only get to see her one weekend a month if I'm lucky. But this was for more than two days. This is Christmas?"

"Yeah. Right." Zack looked down at the floor, his jaw twitching. "Bottom-line it, Mike. Tell me straight out what you want."

"A compromise. Let's meet in four days on December twenty-eighth. Hell, we've closed the corporate offices until January second. So if we meet with George then, we'll get the work done in half the time than it would be otherwise, and without interruption. Then I can leave and spend a couple more days in New York, if I'm lucky."

Zack heard Mike muttering to himself as he turned and began his charge down the stairs. He was an emotional train wreck. Probably because the guy was so out of shape. For crying out loud, he heard him gasping for breath with every step they took right behind him. On the third floor landing, Zack turned and glanced back at him, deciding to give the wimp a breather. "Okay, you can have until the twenty-eighth, but on one condition. You read the draft annual report and edit it between now and then."

"Deal. I'll pick it up later."

"Why not get it now and then take off? Come on, let's head up and get it."

Mike glanced up the stairwell. "Tell you what, I'll meet you there." He grabbed the doorknob to the hall and the waiting elevator and turned back to him, smiling. "In fact, I'll bet I beat you."

"Coward."

"Wrong. I've reached my peak heart rate."

Zack continued to climb. He had to get that

boy in a habit of going to the gym with him every day.

****

"Crandall, my plane leaves in ten minutes."

Charging down Concourse-B of San Francisco Airport, Crandall stared back at Gretta's red face. Why was she even trying to keep up the pace? Gretta was the one who had a plane to catch, and if she kept slogging along like this, she wouldn't make it. The woman wouldn't make it two miles in a marathon. "Look, I need to review the changes to the ad campaign. Since reading that book on branding, I'm not sure we've positioned ourselves right. Pretzelicious is sagging, and we're still in danger of a hostile takeover by Washington Enterprises. Believe me, Gretta, you don't want any part of working with their worthless leader."

Gretta bit her lip and looked at Crandall like she might start crying. She hoped the woman wasn't going through peri-menopause.

"Crandall, honey, you can read through all

our plans and I'll make changes as necessary after Christmas. The due date for the TV blitz isn't 'til February first. So stop worrying. There's plenty of time for tweaks."

"Not if I'm going to stay on schedule and roll out my new Cherry-Lemon Margarita pretzelin January." She stopped short and squared her shoulders. Be damned if anything was going to stand in the way of a spectacular debut and soaring profits to keep Xavier Washington's hands off what belonged to her.

"Look," Gretta said, "I'm already fifteen minutes late for my gate due to being one of the lucky ones who got searched. I promise, Crandall, I'll look at your changes between Christmas and New Year's. Fair enough?"

Crandall broke into a smile. She knew she'd ultimately have it her way. "As long as I can have them before the first. You know how I am about my deadlines. I promised myself I'd have everything finished by the end of the week. Is the twenty-eighth okay with you?"

Gretta looked like she was biting nails in

half. The woman was way too tense. Another reason she needed more exercise. Thank God Gretta was getting a few days off, because she apparently had difficulty handling the normal hustle and bustle of Crandall Drake's world. But she had a hell of a creative flair, so Crandall had long ago decided to grin and bear it.

"Don't you have plans for Christmas?" Gretta asked. "I mean, someone special to spend it with and relax. You know, unwind?"

Crandall blinked in surprise, then slowly shook her head. Gretta was staring at her like she pitied her. She felt her ire rise up like the hair on an irritated cat. "Well, no, not really. It's just me and my tropical fish. Most animals shed you know. Not good if you don't like to vacuum. Not only that, I just sold my condo. It went months faster than I thought, and now the new owners want to close earlier than I expected. I have to find a place to stay before my new house is ready the beginning of March." Crandall tapped her chin with her forefinger. "I have it until after the holiday, but then...I don't suppose you have room in your apartment?"

Gretta cleared her throat. "Uh, Crandall, Mike's planning to visit. I'm not sure how long he'll be there. Then, I'm not sure about..."

"Mike, oh yeah. Forget I said anything." Crandall was consumed by a bleak feeling of total loneliness. Why did the holidays always do this to her? She supposed it was the price she had to pay for her job. "Look, do you think you can finish any changes I have before New Year's?"

Gretta nodded her head, still not meeting Crandall's eyes. "Oh yeah. As long as it's not a total start at the beginning kind of thing. Plenty of time. I'll fit it in between Christmas dinner and opening presents."

"Huh?"

"Never mind."

The loud speaker activated directly over their heads. "Last call for Flight 223 to New York."

Crandall watched as Gretta scrunched her

lips together and slung her carry-on out in the air like she was ready to drop-kick it. No way would she close the distance in time. "I'm sorry you missed your flight, Gretta."

"Give me a minute." Gretta whipped out her cell phone, dialed her travel agent, and ten minutes later, she turned and smiled at Crandall. "I'm rebooked on a flight leaving in an hour. I'd better get to my gate and check-in. Wouldn't want to miss this flight, too."

"Right. And look on the bright side, this gives us more time to work on the campaign."

CHAPTER TWO

February First

"Gotta leave it to Magic." Tom Kreger leaned forward on his barstool and scooped up another giant oyster. Just like everything else in Texas, Gulf oysters were bigger. "As always, he knows how to pick 'em."

Grinning, Tom studied the Gulf through the windows of Cocoanuts. For a first visit to Texas in winter, this was turning out to be a dandy vacation.

The flight into Austin had been smooth and on time. The drive down to South Padre had been fast and free of traffic. Yep, being on the waterfront of South Padre Island sure as hell beat Philadelphia in February. The fact the hated snow hardly ever fell here was just an added bonus.

Tom tipped another oyster to his mouth and promised himself that he was moving south. All it would take was one more year with Maxwell, and he'd have the money. Maybe not for down here, but hopefully he could find a spot in Austin. If not there, then in the rolling hills that surrounded the city.

Keep your nose clean, Kreger, and do what Maxwell tells you. No screw-ups, Kreger, no matter how weird the assignment.

He glanced around the bar. Where was the old codger? It wasn't like him to be late for their appointments. Then again, it wasn't like he was an expert on Maxwell. He'd only worked for him one year and, even then, had only a few meetings with the guy.

Suddenly, people began to turn, and Tom knew why.

Maxwell was in all his gaudy glory, and, as usual impervious to the stares he received as he crossed the room.

Tom shook his head. Well, at least the white Stetson, tank top, shorts, and a pair of ostrich quill cowboy boots weren't as bad as some of his outfits last year. Still, as Maxwell eased onto the stool beside him, Tom, in spite of his best efforts, grinned.

"Hi there, boy. Sorry I'm late. Been practicing at the pool tables. There's a tournament coming up in a couple of days."

"Pool tables?"

"Yep. Haven't played eight ball in a few years. Haven't really cared since Fats died."

"Fats?"

Maxwell clapped his hands in front of Tom's face. "Get with it boy. Minnesota Fats. The best there ever was."

"You knew him?"

"Yep. Don't tell me you haven't heard of him?"

"Sure I've heard of Minnesota Fats. It's just

that he seems like Elvis, a legend, but not someone you *know*."

Maxwell laughed and ordered a bottled water. He leaned forward and exposed a tuft of gray hair on his barrel chest. "Fats was special. A real kidder and a great pool player. You would've liked him. Elvis was another matter. Oh, well, at least he knew how to treat his mother."

"Right. You knew both Fats and Elvis."

"Yep. By the way, with Elvis, I didn't match him and Priscilla. But I guess you'd figure that one out seeing how they divorced."

Tom chuckled. "Right. Not Elvis and Priscilla. Only the really great ones like Paul Newman and Joanne Woodward, Bill and Camille Cosby, Phil Donohue and Marlo Thomas..."

"Exactly! You're learning fast. Now, down to business."

Tom swiveled his chair so he faced Maxwell. "I'm ready. What're we going to do this year, boss?"

"You tell me, boy." Maxwell crossed his legs and pumped his booted foot. "I placed my ad in all the world newspapers January first just as I always do. I included the usual stuff, you know, 'please send me information on a friend or family in dire need of love that will last forever.' Got near a million replies this year. But right there, smack dab in the middle of them all, was one from a woman named Gretta. Funny thing about what she wrote me. Seems you gave the go-ahead for her to write me about a match."

Tom closed his eyes and cursed silently. Nothing like screwing up a good thing before you got started.

"Um, about that. I didn't think she had a chance when I told her she could use my name in the letter. I mean, with the millions you get ...." At Maxwell's stare, he glanced away. "Gretta helped me a long time ago. I ... err. I was a stupid kid in foster care, separated from my sister and only living kin, who thought he still lived on the right side of the tracks. She saved me from getting killed by the rest of the kids in our foster home. Let's say she's more like my big sister than my real one is, despite the fact she's younger than I am."

Tom picked up another oyster, tipped it to his mouth and swallowed. He hoped the mollusk added good fortune, not just stamina. "Gretta deserves a little happiness. And her boyfriend Mike's the perfect man."

Maxwell chucked Tom lightly under the chin, then touched the side of his nose. "Magic knows everything. Despite the fact Ms. Fishman is your friend and the fact that the woman she wants matched is another insecure female like our last match, how can I object? The two people your friend, Gretta, wrote me about are in such dire need of assistance." He shook his head. "In fact, I'd say they're one of the most dysfunctional couples I've ever seen, yet alone matched."

"If even half of what Gretta has said is true, I agree."

Maxwell rubbed his hands together and

laughed. "This one's special. This'll be better than last year. By the way, our last match had twins."

"I saw it on TV." Tom took a swig of his beer. "I haven't gotten a chance to thank you for my Christmas present, the tree, stocked refrigerator, and the box of classics. Not to mention the diet Dr. Peppers. How did you do it?"

"You'll figure it out in time." Maxwell winked. "Remember, last year I suggested you read *The Gift of the Magi*?"

"I read it Christmas day. You were right, it fit our couple."

"Glad to see you got it. This year you should read *Jane Eyre*."

Tom brushed the hair out of his face. "Why that one?"

"Love is often a sacrifice, son. This one will be, too. Tell your Gretta and her Mr. Kramer to get those two down to a little island near South Padre. Fact is, I own it." He snickered. "Very elite, as in only a few people can get reservations." He winked. "Intervention number two explains what the two will do once they get there. But first, you get a chance to play Doctor."

"What?"

"Not really, but you need to give Mike a little powder to slip into Zack's drink. He'll think he's pushing his health. Don't worry, you'll do fine." Maxwell shook his head. "But the interventions aren't easy." He fished in his pocket and handed one sheet of folded notebook paper to Tom.

Tom slowly unfolded it, read it, then placed the list on the bar. "And I thought the first year was bad." He mopped his forehead with a handkerchief.

"Don't worry about the interventions, boy. They'll work. You've just got to believe."

I hope you enjoyed my books and the excerpts. Come see more about my books at www.DarynCross.com, www.BobbyeTerry-MysteryHappens.com and www.BobbyeTerry.com .

Daryn Cross

Also known as Bobbye Terry

www.ingramcontent.com/pod-product-compliance
Lightning Source LLC
Chambersburg PA
CBHW070804180626
46818CB00001B/93